THE BOY WHOSE WISHES CAME TRUE is the second book by Helen Rutter, author of THE BOY WHO MADE EVERYONE LAUGH, which was shortlisted for the Blue Peter Best Story Award and the Costa Children's Book Award, among many other prizes. It was one of the bestselling debut children's books of 2021 and was described by Jacqueline Wilson as "Very funny, very touching, very truthful – a total delight to read."

Helen lives in the countryside just outside Sheffield with her comedian husband, two children and two dogs, Ronnie and Billy Whizz. When she is not tapping away in her writing room, she loves walking the dogs, playing board games and reading.

PRAISE FOR
THE BOY WHO MADE EVERYONE LAUGH

"Truly, a heart-tugger of a book. Between the jokes is an incredibly moving and uplifting portrayal of one boy's struggle to find his voice. In Billy Plimpton, Helen Rutter has created a wonderfully real and inspiring character who reminds us of the importance of kindness."
Jenny Pearson, bestselling author of
The Miraculous Journey of Freddie Yates

"This book is a great way of showing children how to be confident by having a sense of humour and making others laugh"
Baroness Floella Benjamin

"Who can resist a bit of funny kindness? Not me!"
Liza Tarbuck

"A laugh out loud story, the like of which I've never read before"
Kerry Godliman

"So funny and joyful"
Rachel Parris

THE BOY WHOSE WISHES CAME TRUE

Helen Rutter

Published in the UK by Scholastic, 2022
Euston House, 24 Eversholt Street, London, NW1 1DB
Scholastic Ireland, 89E Lagan Road, Dublin Industrial Estate,
Glasnevin, Dublin, D11 HP5F

SCHOLASTIC and associated logos are trademarks and/or
registered trademarks of Scholastic Inc.

ISBN 978 0702 30086 8

A CIP catalogue record for this book
is available from the British Library.

Printed by CPI Group (UK) Ltd, Croydon, CR0 4YY
Paper made from wood grown in sustainable forests
and other controlled sources.

1 3 5 7 9 10 8 6 4 2

www.scholastic.co.uk

For my mum

CHAPTER ONE

**You always have to believe in your dreams.
—Lucas Bailey, star striker of Valley Rovers**

**I dreamed last night that I was being eaten
by a giant hamster. —Archie Crumb**

My mum used to tell me to make wishes all the time. At all the usual things – blowing out candles on a cake, catching a dandelion clock in the air, spotting a rainbow – but there were a million other reasons to wish too.

If we said something at the exact same time:

"Make a wish!"

If we ever saw a feather, or a bird of any kind – even a scabby, one-legged pigeon:

"Make a wish, Archie!"

Even the most disgusting things:

"Ergh, Mum, there's one of your hairs in my fried egg!"

"Make a wish, Archie. Quick!"

"Erm ... I wish there wasn't a hair in my fried egg?!"

If we walked under a bridge when a train went by, if I bumped my elbow, if wind blew leaves into my face or if snow started falling. Every single thing was worth a wish, according to my mum.

"If you don't wish for it, then it can't come true, can it?"

When you have to make so many wishes, it's hard to know what to wish for. I went through all of the usual things: becoming a millionaire, being able to fly, more wishes, cool trainers. None of those wishes came true – I don't think they ever do. Not mine anyway.

My name is Archie Crumb and I'm a pretty useless person. I'm one of those kids who can't really do anything, and I mean ANYTHING. Most people, if they are not so good at something like maths, are usually pretty good at another thing like art. Those kids who are rubbish at school lessons generally head out into the playground at lunch and can run really fast or jump super high or score every goal in football.

Even Felix Ratton in my class, who is worse than me at spelling, can take a lawnmower apart and put it back together again. We didn't know that till he won a prize at the school fair. The prize was to be the teacher for a day (sounds more like a punishment than a prize, if you ask me!). Everyone thought Felix would be a terrible teacher, but it was the best day ever! He told us he has six lawnmowers at home that he found in skips or by people's bins. He took them home and fixed them. Apparently he's always on the lookout for a broken lawnmower. He can even recognize the make by its sound. None of us knew anything about his love for lawnmowers until the day he became our teacher.

The day after Felix's lesson, when I was at my dad's, I tried to take his brand-new lawnmower apart and put it back together again, to see if that was my hidden talent too. I ended up sweating, surrounded by bits of metal and screws with absolutely no idea where any of them were meant to go. Dad and Julie were furious. Lawnmowers are definitely not my secret gift. I still haven't found out what is, and I'm starting to lose hope.

Teachers always say that everyone is good at something. Not me. I come bottom in EVERYTHING.

I have absolutely no special skills. I'm bad at every lesson, I can't do my times tables, my spelling is hideous, my handwriting looks like spiders and the last time I drew my mum a picture she thought it was a teapot when it was meant to be a ship. Why on earth would I have been drawing a teapot?! I can't run in a straight line without falling over, let alone kick a ball properly. I'm even rubbish at computer games.

Mum doesn't bother telling me to wish any more, not now that she's in bed. Most of the time she's asleep – or pretending to be. I know when she's pretending; it's all down to the breathing. I used to do that too, when I was little. The trick is to breathe super slowly. When I get in from school and put my head round the door, I can see her eyes closed, just above the duvet, but I can see her breath making the covers go up and down, too fast for real sleep.

I'm not sure why she pretends. I think maybe she's too tired to talk. That's OK – I just go and sort out my football stickers and eat spaghetti hoops straight out of the tin.

Sometimes I take my spaghetti and snuggle up in bed too, with my stickers, making lists of who I need to get and who I have already got. I love the red, shiny packets and I know all of the stats and facts about the players. On the back of every packet is where I get all my best inspirational quotes. A bit like the pictures Julie has in the living room that say LIVE LAUGH LOVE – but better. I love these quotes – expecially the Lucas Bailey ones – and I always try to follow their advice, but sometimes it doesn't work out.

How can you follow your dreams if you don't even know what your dreams are? I have no idea what I want to do with my life, and I can't understand how other kids seem to already know – we're only eleven! Everyone seems to have it all worked out: Mouse wants to be a lawyer, Martha wants to be a dog groomer, Kiran wants to be an ice-skater and most of the boys want to be footballers.

There is no chance of me EVER being a footballer and so I'll stick with my stickers – get it? *Stick* with my *stickers*! I have a HUGE pile of doubles, probably the biggest in the school. Some kids do the most stupid swaps, like fifty doubles for one shiny, but I love my doubles pile. I keep all of my Lucases together in a separate pile. I have fifty-two Lucas Baileys. He's my favourite. Last season he scored thirty-five goals and was the top scorer. He's from round here too; he used to go to my school. There are pictures of him all over the corridors and a massive display in reception with newspaper clippings and interviews he's done.

Sometimes I talk to him. I know it sounds stupid and I get a bit scared that talking to a sticker might mean that I'm bonkers – but I do. If stickers had little ears and could hear then he would know so much about me. He would know that Mouse is my best friend and that she's better at football than any of the other girls at school and most of the boys too – if she was given a chance. We practise penalties in her garden, and I have NEVER seen her miss one. She's amazing.

He would know that the B-B Gang are horrible and say mean things about EVERYONE. He would know that I cheated and looked at Martha's maths test today. He would also know that I then felt so bad and so worried, I scribbled all of the answers out and got zero out of twenty.

He would know that nine is my lucky number because it's the number on his shirt, and that sometimes I say things nine times in my head to try and make them happen or tap things on the table nine times to bring me good luck. He would be the only person in the world who knows that Mum has only got out of bed once this week.

She'll get better; she says she just needs time. I know she's trying. She booked us a holiday to Scarborough last Easter and we spent weeks talking about the slot machines and the sea. Then the week before we were meant to go, she started staying in bed again. Longer and longer. Saying how much her head hurt. I knew straight away that the holiday was off. The day before we were meant to get the train she was crying and saying how bad she felt. I ended up having to tell her that it was OK even though it didn't feel OK.

That's sometimes what happens with Mum: she steals all the feelings so there are none left for me. There was the time that I was meant to have a proper birthday party sleepover with popcorn and a movie. We'd tidied up the house and everything. The day I was taking invites into school she went very shaky and said that she was not ready to have a house full of people and so I just went to Mouse's for my birthday tea instead.

There's always a reason why she can't go to every single school play, sports day and parents' evening. It's just the way it is; it's not her fault, is it? She doesn't want to be like this. So why do I sometimes feel so angry with her?

Mum says I'm not allowed to tell anyone that she stays in bed. They'll get all worried and involved and that's the last thing she needs. If she's too tired to chat to *me* some days, then imagine how bad it would be if we had teachers ringing her all the time.

When I go to Dad's, he'll say, "How's your mum?" but I know it's not a real question. There are loads of questions that aren't real. Sometimes I see grown-ups pass each other on the street and say, "Hi. You all right?" without even stopping to hear the answer – that's not a real question, is it, so what's the point in asking it? It's the same with Dad. He doesn't want the real answer and so I always just say, "The same."

That seems to satisfy him. I don't want to lie and that feels like the truth – but not the whole truth. I HATE lying. My dad's a liar. When I was seven, he told me the biggest lie ever. I heard him and Mum shouting in the kitchen and when I went downstairs, he told me not to worry.

"Everything's going to be OK, Archie," he said.

Well, it wasn't. They kept shouting in the kitchen for months, until one day he left. Now he's married to Julie, who has shiny skin and dangly earrings. They had my sister, Scadge, who he clearly loves way more than me. That's when Mum started feeling bad and needing to rest. A year ago she lost her job and so now she has nothing to get out of bed for anyway.

Everything was not "OK". So now I don't really

believe anything he says.

I go to Dad and Julie's house every other weekend. I like going so I can see Scadge, even though she's spoiled rotten and gets anything she wants. She really makes me laugh. She's three. Her name is actually Scarlett, but I call her Scadge. Julie HATES it.

"Archie, please don't call her that. It makes her sound like an urchin."

Scadge loves it though. Whenever Julie tells me off, she sings, "Scadgy Scadgy Scadgy scoo!" and makes farting sounds with her tongue.

"Delightful!" Julie always says, and me and Scadge just burst out laughing and carry on singing the Scadge song.

She's completely obsessed with unicorns; her whole bedroom is covered in them and it always smells like sherbet. Julie puts her in frilly white dresses and only lets her play with one toy at a time.

It's my weekend with Dad now. Today, when I get there, I take Scadge into the perfect back garden, which looks like every blade of grass has been trimmed with hairdressing scissors, and teach her how to kick a football. She's the only person in the world who I can beat at football. She loves it and squeals every time she tries to kick the ball.

Then she gets overexcited and starts squealing and dancing, falls over the ball, gets mud all over her dress, and of course I get into trouble.

"What on earth do you look like, Scarlett Rose! Well, thank you, Archie, thank you very much!" Julie snaps. "Now, go and get changed and find something tidy to do."

Scadge goes up to get changed and fetch a unicorn board game for us to play and Dad goes into the kitchen. Which leaves me and Julie on our own.

I feel big in their house, even though I'm actually pretty small. I end up knocking things over and spilling drinks and then there's a flurry of panic to get it all perfect again. So far I haven't broken anything or bumped into anything this weekend, but there's still time.

I don't think Julie likes my visits much. She always looks really uncomfortable and if we're ever left in a room alone together, she makes this sound like a cross between a laugh and a sigh. She makes that noise now.

"Hah'mmmm."

I'm not sure what the noise means but it makes me feel weird. Am I meant to do the noise back to her? Or say something? Or just sit in the weird silence that follows it?

After a bit of awkward breathing in and out I say the first thing that pops into my head.

"How come your sofa smells so sweet?"

Julie's whole face lights up.

"I use a fifty-fifty mix of fabric conditioner and water, in a little spray bottle. Here!" She takes a pretty glass bottle out of a drawer and asks if I want to "give it a squirt".

I take the bottle. It is shaped like a cloud and is made out of beautiful clear glass with blue swooshes through it. It looks like it should hold expensive perfume, not just sofa spray. I hold it out carefully, and after feeling the shape of the bottle and staring at the pattern in the glass I give it a squirt.

"The fabric conditioner is called Summer Breeze and it is my favourite smell ever," she says. She closes her eyes and breathes in deeply. She looks really happy and relieved now that we have found something to talk about.

As I sit there smelling the Summer Breeze, I wonder how many other eleven-year-old boys Julie has met. I'm guessing not many.

The next time I do a food shop I'm going to look for some Summer Breeze fabric conditioner so that our sofa smells as good as Julie's. It'll probably be too expensive though. I've tried to clean our house and make it sparkle, but it never does. There are stains on the carpet from where I spilled some tomato soup and it always smells a bit disgusting, no matter what I do.

When I'm at home, I can't smell the badness. It's when I go out and come back in again that I notice it. I'm not sure why that happens. Maybe I get used to whatever is rotten and my brain makes it disappear, like magic.

After I've let Scadge beat me three times at her new game, Julie calls us in for lunch. There are matching plates, and the cutlery all has red spotty handles. Scadge is chattering on about how she beat me.

"Next time you come round, Archibald, I will beat you again and again and again!" she says, cackling.

I wish I had never told her that some people called Archie are actually called Archibald. She's not stopped calling me it ever since. Dad laughs too. But then he clears his throat and pulls his serious face, and I know something bad is coming.

"Talking of next time, Archie..." There's a pause as he eats some noodles. "I'm afraid we're going to have to rearrange the weekend after next."

I know what "rearranging" means – it means

cancelling. Dad is constantly "rearranging" our weekends. He doesn't look at me as he slurps up a dangling noodle.

"Julie's friend has offered us their caravan in Wales for the weekend, so we couldn't say no."

Julie makes the weird noise again, "Hah'mmmm," and we all sit there feeling weird. Even Scadge is quiet for once. Our cutlery clinks on our plates.

Then I say in a voice that comes out louder and far less casual than I want, "Can I come too?"

"Yes!" shouts Scadge, dropping her spoon into her bowl.

"I want Archibald to come too! Then I can take my game and beat him again and again and again."

Dad blinks, then he ruffles her hair.

"He can't, sweetie," he says. He's pretending to talk to Scadge, but I know he's really talking to me. "We would all love for him to come but the caravan's really tiny, and he is a big lad now. I'm sure he wouldn't want to be squished in with us for a whole weekend!"

The truth is that I would love to be squished in and, just as I'm about to say so, I knock my fork out of my bowl and send it flying towards the gleaming white tiles. Julie sucks her breath in and starts making little tweeting sounds as she flaps about and cleans it up.

"See, Scarlett, Archie in a caravan would just not work!" Then Dad chuckles and ruffles my hair too, as if everything's sorted.

"So, shall I come next weekend instead?" I ask. Dad darts a glance at Julie.

"Well, it's Scarlett's birthday next weekend…" he says slowly.

"Pleeeease!" begs Scadge.

"Erm…"

"Pleeeeeeeease!"

Dad looks at Julie again, who shrugs and gives a little nod.

"Of course you should come. What a good idea!" Dad says cheerfully, but it feels like he doesn't really think it's such a good idea at all. After a few seconds Julie makes the laugh/sigh sound again.

"Hah'mmmm."

All of a sudden, I feel like I want to get out of this house with its shiny surfaces and sweet smell. I can't wait until four o'clock, when I can ride over to Mouse's for tea.

I don't want to think I'm not welcome at my dad's house. I tell myself that it's all in my head and that they don't mean to make me feel this way. I focus on how much Scadge loves me and how much fun we have. But when I see Dad and Julie look at each other like that – when I see the panic in their eyes at the thought of dealing with me for two weekends in a row – I know that this will never feel like a home for me.

The problem is that my real home doesn't feel like a home either. Proper homes don't smell bad and have someone in bed pretending to sleep all the time, do they? So I'm not sure where that leaves me.

CHAPTER TWO

Even when we hit rock bottom, we can still gaze up at the stars. —Lucas Bailey

The glow-in-the-dark stars on my ceiling stopped working years ago, so now I'm just gazing at plastic. —Archie Crumb

I spend the rest of the afternoon hiding in my room. When I say "my room" I mean the spare room that I sleep in when I'm here.

It's painted white and has an exercise bike in the corner, a huge gym ball – which I bounce around on – great big mirrors on the wall and a huge pink, glittery picture, in a silver frame, that says:

Be the girl who decided to go for it

The picture makes me feel worse than ever.

I lie on the bed looking up at the sparkly words and wonder if Dad and Julie ever even considered that it might not be the best picture to put on the bedroom wall of an eleven-year-old boy. Ages ago they said that they would take me shopping for a duvet cover and some posters, to make it feel like my room, but it never happened. They couldn't make it any more obvious that this is definitely NOT my room. Sometimes Julie accidentally calls it "the gym" and then has to quickly correct herself.

"Sweetie, could you grab the hoover from the gym ... I mean, Archie's room, when you're up there?"

After ten minutes of lying there, I can't look at the stupid picture any more. I stand up and take it off the wall. When it comes off the hook it's heavier than I expected and it slips towards me. I can feel my fingers losing their grip and before I can catch it, it falls to the floor.

I almost can't look. I kneel down on the thick

carpet and wonder if there is a chance that it's not broken.

As I slowly peek under the frame, I can see it – a long crack the whole way from the top to the bottom. There is no way that I'm about to go and tell Julie and Dad what I've done, so I prop it up facing the wall and wedge the gym ball over it, hoping that Julie won't want to work out for a few days. At least I won't have to look at the stupid thing any more!

I head off an hour early to Mouse's – she won't mind and Dad and Julie don't even notice. They're probably just pleased to see me go.

I have Sunday tea at Mouse's every week. We watch Saturday's match on catch-up and me and Mouse shout and scream at the screen and I LOVE it. I used to watch football with Dad but Julie doesn't like it, so that was the end of that.

Mouse's house is the total opposite to Dad and Julie's. Full to the brim with stuff, but nice stuff, not just empty packets and mess like my house. Their shelves are full of photos, snow globes and things that Mouse made at school. Their fridge is covered in magnets and paintings and they have so many pets that the floor is littered with guinea pig hutches and dog beds.

My favourite is Flump, the little white albino

gerbil. Every time I go round, I sit Flump on my knee and she burrows into my pocket or up my sleeve. I wish my mum would let me have a pet. All I want is a little gerbil like Flump, but Mum says, "You're not stinking out the house with rodents. They are full of disease." Sometimes I wonder if she'd even notice. I could get one anyway and keep it in my room. She hasn't been in my room for months.

Altogether, Mouse and her family have twenty-three animals, including fish. Mouse says that they're all her furry brothers and sisters. Their house feels full. The radio's always on and her mum and dad are usually chatting or singing or whistling. Her mum, Zoe, is into yoga and meditation, and tonight when I get there, I can hear her making weird noises in the living room.

"What's she doing?" I whisper to Mouse as I listen to the strange sounds coming through the door.

"Chanting," Mouse says.

"Why?" I ask.

"She thinks about something and then sends 'messages of positivity' out into the universe. She says if you put good stuff out you get good stuff back."

"What about bad stuff?" I say.

She shrugs. "Same, I guess."

That sends a shiver down my spine.

Does that mean that I've put bad stuff out into the universe and that's why I get bad stuff back? Maybe if I put good stuff into the universe, I would have been invited to the caravan?

Mouse takes me into the kitchen and makes us some squash. I listen to Zoe's chanting and watch the cordial mixing with the water. I can feel myself heading into "Archie Land". That's what Mum and Dad used to call it when I was little and used to zone out.

Calling Archie. Earth to Archie Land.

Good time in Archie Land? Did you send us a postcard?

I spend a lot of time in Archie Land these days.

Last week I went into Archie Land when I was meant to be getting changed after swimming. Everyone else left and got on the minibus but I didn't even notice. I was untying my trunks slowly and then tying them again. After twenty minutes Mrs Mather came storming into the changing room. I was still sitting in my trunks, tying and untying the cords together over and over again.

"What on earth have you been doing?" Mrs Mather had said.

"Getting dressed?"

"Archie, the lesson finished ages ago. The minibus is waiting – everyone is on it already."

I shrugged and she sighed and said, "Come on, slowcoach."

I had to get on the minibus wrapped in my towel. The B-B Gang just loved that.

> *"Naked Archie Crumb,*
> *Gets dressed by his mum.*
> *Or he's just so dumb*
> *He's showing off his bum!"*

That song was on repeat for the rest of the week.

Archie Land can really annoy people, like Mrs Mather, but some people find it interesting. Zoe always wants to know what I'm thinking when I "go off".

"Is it like an imaginary land with animals and stuff?" she once asked as we sat eating dinner. I had been flying a piece of spaghetti through the air for ten minutes, while they all watched me and giggled.

"Not really. I'm not thinking of anything in particular. It's like empty space."

"Buddhist monks can put themselves into a deep

state of meditation like that, but most people can't. It's amazing, Archie. You just need to know how to control it, so you don't get into trouble because, unlike a monk, you have to go to school."

I like Zoe. She wears long dresses and usually has gardening gloves on. She's known me my whole life and always has the best juice in the fridge. The stuff with bits in, that tastes like you're on holiday.

Mum and Zoe used to be friends when we were little, but when Mum got bad she started sending messages to people telling them to leave her alone. I know because I saw one when I was plugging her phone in to charge – it had a bad swear word in it. After a while people stopped trying. There are only so many times you'll let someone swear at you in a text, I guess. Zoe still does try every now and then. She sends a note with me or says that she tried calling, but Mum doesn't answer her phone any more.

When I come back from Archie Land, Mouse's dad has come into the kitchen and is cooking something that smells delicious. The radio's on and he's whistling along. My house always seems so quiet. We don't even have a radio to put on. Sometimes I leave the telly on in the background when I'm making my tea to try and make it feel a bit busier. It makes the house seem even more empty somehow. Once I tried to sing to myself when I was making toast but my voice is terrible and so I went bright red, as if someone was listening, and stopped.

Zoe comes through and ruffles my and Mouse's hair. When her dad looks over he pretends to feel left out and lowers his bald head, so she pretends to ruffle his non-existent hair too and they all giggle. Dinner is shepherd's pie and it's delicious. Afterwards me and Mouse go and watch the match – Valley Rovers win 3–0! Then it's time for me to go home. Zoe puts the leftovers into a dish for me. "It'll save your mum from having to cook," she says. She hesitates a minute. "Give my love to her, won't you? Tell her to give me a call any time, I'd love to catch up!" I nod as I take the dish, knowing Mum won't pick up the phone.

As I step out into the cold air Mouse shouts, "Don't forget the maths test tomorrow!"

As she waves and closes the door I can see her mum and dad through the frosty glass, chatting and laughing. I'd forgotten all about the maths test.

I never want to go home on Sunday nights. I feel so warm and full and I don't want to go back to the house. Especially not tonight. Mum was really bad when I left yesterday; her whole face was red and blotchy and she didn't answer when I said bye. I wonder if I will always feel this way about going home.

Then I think about what Mouse said, about sending messages of positivity out into the universe, putting good stuff out there to get good stuff back.

I try to think positively but it's really hard. How do you send something out to the universe anyway? All that keeps popping into my head is Summer Breeze fabric conditioner. I decide to just go with it. I stand in the freezing air, holding on to the warm pie, close my eyes and think about fabric conditioner. I can almost smell it. I imagine my thoughts floating up into the sky.

Maybe if I can get some Summer Breeze I can try and make everything shiny and smelly at home and I can put the shepherd's pie in the oven and turn the telly on and it won't be so lonely.

That's about as much positive thinking as I can manage today. I send it out to the universe and jump on my bike.

I'm riding down the cobbled path, trying to balance the pie on my handlebars, aiming to dodge all of the biggest stones, when my wheel hits a hidden pothole. Everything goes into slow motion and the pie flies into the air with me following it over the handlebars. I see the dish break into two on the ground in front of me and I have a split second to feel bad and wonder how I'm going to tell Zoe that I broke her pie dish, before my head hits the ground and everything goes black.

CHAPTER THREE

Yesterday is the past. Tomorrow is unknown.
Today is your best chance to make a
difference. —Lucas Bailey

I don't even know what day it is?!
—Archie Crumb

When I come round my face feels warm and I try to
open my eyes, but everything is blurry and I panic. It
takes me a moment to realize that I'm covered in pie.

I sit up and wipe my face. That's when I see that
someone is standing over me.

They're hazy at first, but then my eyes focus in on
the red-and-white stripes. It's a sports kit of some
kind. I blink hard and then see it clearly: the Valley
Rovers kit. I look down and see a pair of dark muscly

legs standing in the signature mismatched boots. *It can't be*, I think, blinking hard again and rubbing my sore head. My eyes scan up to his smiling face and I see a person who I never ever thought I would see, apart from on a sticker.

Lucas Bailey.

Leaning over me, in his full kit, smiling, with his hand held out to help me up. It is actually LUCAS BAILEY! This cannot be happening! This really CANNOT be happening.

"That looks tasty!" actual Lucas Bailey says, gesturing to the pie on the ground and grabbing my hand to pull me up.

"Help yourself," I say. "But it tastes better off a plate!"

He laughs. "That was a big fall, buddy. You OK?"

"Yeah," I say, scraping as much potato from my eyelids as I can. I look at the mess on the ground. "The dish isn't. And it doesn't belong to me," I add, picking up the two broken pieces.

"I love that!" He chuckles. "More worried about the dish than your own head!"

He's exactly as I imagined he would be. It's almost like he's come out of my imagination and on to the pavement.

After a few seconds of staring at him I ask, "What are you doing here?"

"I grew up round here, didn't I?" He points down the road, as if it's completely normal for him to be wandering around in his football kit late on a Sunday night. "Right, the dish is a goner. I'll walk you back in case you get dizzy."

As we start walking down the path, me pushing my bike and him carrying the broken pie dish, I look at him again, standing so close, close enough to touch. This can't be happening, can it? I must have hit the ground pretty hard. Maybe I'll wake up in a hospital with bandages around my head and this will all have been just a dream.

I push that thought away though, as I want this to last as long as possible. I want so much for it to be real. We keep walking over the cobbles, his studs clicking and clacking on the stones. We're quiet for a while but not in an awkward way. Not in a way that would need a sigh/laugh to fill it. In a comfortable, easy way. Isn't it weird how silence can be filled with something invisible that makes it feel a certain way? How one silence can feel totally different to another, even though they're both just silence?

"You played **so** well yesterday. That second goal

was incredible," I say as we cross the road and I catch a glimpse of Valley Stadium, peeking over the houses.

"Ah, thanks, buddy. Do you play?"

"Yeah, but I'm rubbish. I never get picked."

"Of course you're rubbish if you never get picked! You have to play to get good. It does my head in when they only pick the best players at school. Everyone can enjoy it so they should let everyone play."

"I know! It's always the same team. My best friend, Mouse, could be one of the best players at school, but she doesn't get picked because she's a girl."

"Mate, that's bad. Tell her to keep going, and you need to keep going too, buddy, even when things are tough."

I don't know why, but then I tell him everything, everything that I've told the sticker version of him, and he just listens. As we pass the house with the gnomes, I tell him that Mum doesn't sing in the shower any more, or do Zumba in the living room. When we get to the postbox, I tell him about Bella, the leader of the B-B Gang, calling me a tramp because my uniform's too small, and about how we can't afford a new one. As we head past the Co-op, I tell him that my dad's going to a caravan in Wales and when I asked if I could come, he told me there wasn't enough space, and that's how it always feels with my dad, like there's not enough space for me in his new life. By the time we get to my front door, Lucas Bailey knows my whole life story.

He stops and looks at me.

"Buddy," he says gently, "I think you need a bit of help."

"I know," I say. "But Mum won't ask anyone—" But before I have time to explain that she's stopped talking to all of her friends and that she won't go to the doctor's or talk to the teachers or anyone, he stops me.

"Not that kind of help."

Then he sits on the kerb and pats the concrete next to him. I sit.

"Sometimes people just need a little bit of luck to come their way. To make them see what's possible. To give them a bit of hope, so that they have the power to change their situation."

"I could definitely use some of that!"

"Well, take it then."

"What do you mean?"

He looks at me and laughs. "You know, I used to look out of my bedroom window and I could see the stadium all lit up at night. For so long I could never imagine myself there. I was too skinny or too naughty. No one ever thought I could do it. It's only when I started believing in myself, really picturing myself on that pitch, that things started to change." Then he looks at me with his kind face and says, "What's your lucky number, Archie Crumb?"

"Nine," I say without hesitating. He nods and turns around to point at the number 9 on his shirt.

"OK, so when you wake up tomorrow, you've got nine wishes, kid. No more, no less. No wishing for more wishes or any of that nonsense. All you have to do is imagine something happening and then wish for it out loud. If you can't imagine it then it won't come true."

I blink at him. "You're joking?"

Lucas shakes his head. "Nope. You can wish for anything you want – but there is one important rule. You can't wish for people to change *inside*. That means you can't wish someone happier or kinder or braver. You have to be specific. You have to be smart about this, Archie."

"If only it was that easy!" I say, looking down at my shoes and remembering all of the wishes I've made that never ever worked.

"If you don't wish for it, then it can't come true, can it?" he says, with laughter still in his eyes.

"That's what my mum used to say!"

But by the time I turn to look at him he's gone. I'm all alone on the pavement, the broken dish sitting on my lap, and as I put my hand to my head, I find a huge lump on my forehead. I feel suddenly exhausted. I realize how strange I must look, sitting alone on a pavement in the dark and covered in gravy and mashed potato. Rain starts to fall. I heave my aching, bruised body up off the kerb and find my key.

As I'm about to open the door, I stop and imagine Mum on the other side, in the kitchen cooking cheesy pasta just like she used to, or watching one of our favourite quiz shows. I picture her smiling up at me as I walk in, the house warm and glowing. Cheesy smells filling the air.

I wish it was true.

But I don't say it. I don't think any amount of magic would make that come true, and so instead I go into the cold, dark house.

CHAPTER FOUR

You are braver than you will ever know.
—Lucas Bailey

You should have heard me scream when I
trod on a slug in bare feet. —Archie Crumb

When I wake the next morning the world feels different somehow. Like the sun is shining brighter and the beep from my football alarm clock is louder than usual.

As I roll over and press the snooze button, I see my Lucas Bailey doubles on my bedside table. I don't remember putting them there and as I pick them up, I get what feels like a static shock from the shiny paper. I drop them on to the duvet and they scatter, his face peering up at me from the bed over and over again. That's when I remember what happened last night.

I can hear his words: *sometimes people just need a little bit of luck to come their way. To make them see what's possible.*

I hold up one of the stickers. "Ha! I must have banged my head pretty hard to bring you to life!"

Then I hear the voice again, but this time it sounds even clearer in my head.

OK, so when you wake up tomorrow, you've got nine wishes, kid. No more, no less.

Then even more clearly, as though he's in the room with me.

All you have to do is imagine something happening and then wish for it out loud.

I stare at his face and then shake my head.

"There is no way that this is real," I say to him. I gather all of the stickers together in a pile. His eyes seem to be watching me, waiting for me to do something.

When I see my maths book poking out of my bag, I feel instantly sick. The maths test. I open the book to see if I understand anything that we're meant to have revised and it all just looks like gobbledygook.

I HATE maths so much. If Mrs Mather ever picks on me to answer a question, or even if she comes around to look over my shoulder as I'm working, my heart beats faster and my neck gets hot. Tests are the absolute worst; I always come bottom. Last week when Mrs Mather handed out the marked tests, I tried to hide my paper, but Bella snatched it and started howling with laughter, saying, "Poor little Archie can't even add up. He'll never be able to afford any trousers that fit him!"

Bella and Bea, otherwise known as the B-B Gang, have been ruining kids' lives since we were in reception. Bella is the boss and Bea is her little sidekick. They have the same swishy blonde hair and always wear the same clothes on non-uniform day. It's a bit weird, if you ask me – maybe wearing the same clothes would seem like fun when you're five, but surely the joy wears off by the time you are eleven? There are a few girls who try and cling to them in the hope that they won't get picked on, but you can often find some poor girl crying in a corner of the playground, having been kicked out of the B-B Gang – it's brutal.

They really started picking on me when they found out that my mum had lost her job. She used to work for Bella's dad's building company, sending emails and answering the phone. Then, after Scadge was born, she got really sad and missed work some days. She got a few warnings and tried really hard to get better but it never worked for long. A year ago they sacked her. That just made it worse.

Bella's dad must have told Bella. I sometimes picture them all around their table eating their roast dinner and talking about us. Since then, the B-Bs have started calling me and Mum lazy tramps.

I try to think about what I really want to do today instead of failing a test and being laughed at by Bella and Bea. I wonder what Lucas Bailey would choose to do. And then I remember reading an interview with him where he was asked that very question.

I jump up and search through my old pile of Premiership magazines. Mouse gives me them when she's read them. She says that her house is so full of stuff that she wants her room to be clear and empty. I suppose everyone wants something they haven't got.

When I find the magazine, I flick through to the interview and there he is, smiling out at me with a football under his arm. Next to the question *What would be your ideal day off?* there is a big speech bubble that says, "I would stay in bed, order pizza and play FIFA on the Xbox all day!"

"I haven't got an Xbox!" I say to the picture staring back at me. "And I definitely don't have enough money to order pizza!" I close the magazine and see the maths book sitting there, taunting me. "OK, Lucas, I'll prove it – wishes just don't come true."

I close my eyes and imagine lying on my bed playing Xbox, surrounded by pizza boxes, and then I do it. I shout my wish to the universe.

"I WISH I COULD STAY IN BED, EAT PIZZA AND PLAY FIFA ON THE XBOX ALL DAY."

I sit on my bed and wait for something magical to happen but, after five minutes of waiting, nothing does. Then the bin lorry starts beeping outside and I can hear the shouts of the bin men and the banging of wheelie-bin lids. I sigh – there is nothing magical about bins.

I pick up one of my Lucas stickers. "I knew it was too good to be true," I say to him. "You're still the greatest footballer who ever lived though, so don't worry too much." Then I pull on my too-small trousers, pop one of my Lucas stickers in my pocket for luck and head downstairs.

As I'm about to head out of the door, I hear Mum's groggy voice from upstairs.

"Archie?"

Sometimes I think Mum puts on that weak, sleepy voice so that I don't get any ideas and think she might be getting better and is going to start cooking meals and doing the shopping again. I'm not daft; if she spoke in a normal voice I wouldn't expect her to skip downstairs and do a dance routine.

"Yeah?" I shout back.

"I just had a text from school, love. It's closed."

I freeze, drop my rucksack on the floor, take Lucas out of my pocket and look right into his eyes. "You didn't?!"

Then I run upstairs and into Mum's room. She smiles at me.

"Good job I checked my phone, isn't it? I normally never switch the thing on! Apparently, the boiler's gone down so it's shut for the day. Lucky you!"

"Yeah, it is pretty lucky," I say, trying to contain the bubble of excitement in my tummy. "Do you want a cuppa?"

"Ooh, I'd love one. And I forgot to say. Next door but two left a box of stuff for you. You know the lady with the yappy dog?"

"What stuff?" I ask.

"No idea. She knocked yesterday, but I was asleep." *Pretending to be asleep*, I think. "She left it out the back."

I run downstairs, nearly falling down the last few steps, and see the cardboard box sitting by the door. There's a note pinned to it.

Dear Archie,

I thought you might get some use out of these things.

James has headed off to uni now (I really miss him!) and says that he doesn't want them any more. Sorry I didn't drop them over sooner, but I have only just got round to going through his stuff.

I hope you and your mum are doing OK? Knock on if you ever need anything.

Rosemary (number 12)

After a big breath in, I fling the flaps open. Inside I can see a whole jumble of stuff. Underneath some juggling clubs there's a remote-control robot and a couple of board games. I'm starting to lose hope. Maybe I was wrong.

Then it happens. Underneath a book on the solar system, it's just sitting there. An old, battered box with brown tape holding the sides together and on the top the word XBOX. I lift up the lid and see an envelope sitting on the console. Inside the envelope is the FIFA game.

I take Lucas out of my pocket. "I take it all back – you are totally magic!" I'm not sure what to do with myself. I pace around holding the Xbox, grinning like an idiot. When my face starts hurting from smiling so much I realize that I need to talk to someone.

"Mouse!" I say as soon as she picks up the phone. "Can you come over?!"

"No, Mum's making me go to the supermarket. What a waste of a day off school."

"I need to see you. Something weird's happened."

"What have you done, Archie? But be quick, Mum's calling me."

"It was all a bit weird," I say, "and I don't know if it was real but today something's happened that makes me think it *was* real. And if it is real then I have eight wishes left."

"What are you on about?!"

Then I hear a rustling.

"Hi, Archie," Zoe says. "I'm afraid Jasmin is all mine today and we're just on our way out of the door. She will see you tomorrow, you can talk to her then. Honestly, I don't know what the pair of you have left to talk about. You see that much of each other."

"But I really need to tell her something."

There's a pause. "Are you OK, Archie?" she says, sounding worried.

"Yeah," I say.

"Is your mum OK? Is she there? I would love to chat to her, it's been so long."

"She's fine," I say. "We're fine. She's in the shower," I lie, instantly feeling bad. "But I really need to talk to Mouse."

"Well, if you're fine and your mum's fine then it can wait until tomorrow, Archie Crumb, or I will never get her out of the house, will I?" Mouse is protesting in the background but I know Zoe won't give in. She's pretty strict when she wants to be.

Once I've put the phone down, I pace again for a while. I don't know what to do with myself. Then I look at my Lucas sticker and the Xbox. "Fine, I'll just do exactly what you would do."

When I take Mum a cup of tea, I ask, "Mum, could I move the telly into my room? Just for today."

"I don't see why not," she says. "I'm feeling rotten anyway – you enjoy yourself."

"Thanks, Mum," I say, and skip down the stairs.

It's actually quite hard carrying a telly upstairs on your own. It's in front of my face so I can't see where I'm going, and our stairs are steep like a ladder. I keep thinking I'm going to overbalance and tip backwards. In my room I'm not sure where all the wires go. I've never had a computer. Scadge has got one, even though she's only three, but it only has stupid games with unicorns and cartoon characters in. That's another thing Mum feels guilty about. Now she's not working we don't have any money for stuff like we used to, not that we ever had that much anyway. She gets a bit of money every week because she hasn't got a job, but that's just for food, not computers.

I asked for an Xbox for Christmas and my birthday last year, but Mum said she couldn't afford it and so I got my bike instead – because she found it going cheap on Facebook. Don't get me wrong, I love my bike, even though it's still a bit too big, and is rusty and dented and has the name "Jack" painted on it. But at the time I was super disappointed.

Me and Mouse call my bike Jack now.

"Are you walking or coming on Jack?"

"I'm coming on Jack so I'll be there in five."

Three hours and loads of FIFA later I've figured out how to pass and shoot, and I'm having a brilliant time. I love how every goal is different and I can picture myself scoring like this in real life. Crossing the ball into the box; flicking it up over the keeper's head and into the back of the net. My celebrations with each goal get bigger and bigger. I throw my teddies into the air, put my T-shirt over my face, shout, cheer and jump on the bed. For the first time I can really imagine what it would be like to be good at football.

I'm just about to start yet another game when I hear a loud knock at the front door. I drop the controller and go down to see who it is. As soon as I open it, I remember the rest of my wish. There is a tall skinny boy standing there in a red jacket holding four huge pizza boxes.

"Mr Jenkins?" he asks, in a bored tone.

"No," I answer. "There's no Mr Jenkins here."

The tall boy huffs and gets his phone out. "Is this 16 Providence Road?"

"Yes."

"Well, a Mr Jenkins ordered pizza to this address."

"What shall we do?" I ask.

"I don't know," he says. "Eat it?" And he plonks the boxes into my arms, jumps back on his moped and whizzes off.

"Pizza for lunch, Mum?" I ask as I peep around the door, but she's either asleep or pretending to be. "It was free!" I whisper as I leave a box on the floor by her bed.

By the end of the day, I'm doing pepperoni burps, feeling sick from pizza and have a FIFA headache. Who would have thought that sitting in bed playing video games and eating two huge pizzas would be so tiring? I get Lucas out of my pocket and shake my head.

"The next wish I make is not going to involve any food, that's for sure." And as I look down at the sticker, I'm sure I can see his eyes laughing back up at me.

What should I wish for next? I try and think about what Lucas said again.

You can't wish for people to change inside.

You have to be smart about this, Archie.

The main thing I want is for Mum to be happier, but I can't wish that. What about money? I could wish for loads and loads of money. Me and Mum could buy a massive house, go on amazing holidays together and have our own bowling alley. But if she hasn't got the energy to answer the phone, she's not about to go to buy a new house and visit Disneyland, is she?! No amount of money would get her out of bed. Anyway, an eleven-year-old carrying around thousands of pounds is pretty suspicious. I don't want to end up trying to explain all this to a policeman. "My wishes are coming true, honest, guv!" Like Lucas says, I have to be smart about this.

Maybe I should wish to be invited to the caravan with Scadge. To be the best footballer in the world. That the B-B Gang vanish into mid-air. My head buzzing with wishes, I carefully tear a page from the middle of my maths book and write at the top:

ARCHIE CRUMB'S WISH LIST

1. XBOX & PIZZA
2.
3.
4.
5.
6.
7.
8.
9.

The blank spaces make me giddy. My whole life could change based on what I write in these spaces. But what on earth am I going to put next to wish number two?

CHAPTER FIVE

Something deep inside tells me to get back up and keep trying. —Lucas Bailey

Something deep inside tells me to do fifteen pepperoni burps and then keep on eating pizza. —Archie Crumb

I'm awake all night running through wish ideas and then deciding that they're silly or won't work. I nearly get up and ring Mouse at midnight. I can't keep it all to myself for a second longer, but then I get distracted by the idea of wishing for my own pet monkey.

The next morning I'm running late as usual and after shoving in a piece of burned toast and downing some squash, I pop my head around Mum's door.

"Bye, Mum," I whisper into the dark.

She's sitting propped up against her pillows, her eyes sad. "See you later, sweetie, have a great day. I'll try and make something nice for tea, eh?"

"Yeah," I reply. "See how you feel."

Mum says this every day, but she never makes something nice for tea. Not recently anyway. On the mornings I stay and chat, she starts talking about all the things we'll do when she's better. I've heard it all before – hundreds of times. We're going to go on our first holiday, we're going to get a puppy, we're going to decorate the house and go for picnics and fly kites and swim in the sea. All when she's better.

It's not that I don't want to hear it all again – I love to imagine all of these things – but when she gets to the end of imagining, she starts feeling sad about how we can't do any of it and then she starts saying sorry and crying and I don't want that at all and so I quickly change the subject.

"Mum?" I say quietly. "If you could wish for anything in the world, what would you wish for?"

"Easy," she says. "For you to be happy. Every time. That's all I ever want."

"OK, thanks, Mum. Will do my best! Love you," I say, thinking that that's no help whatsoever. I can't just wish to "be happy". I need to think about things that will **make** me happy. That way Mum might be happy too.

As I pass the postbox, I remember Lucas standing next to me on the cobbles, his arm brushing against mine, and when I see the gnomes it's like I can feel him walking by my side again. It's nice, like I'm not so alone. When I get to Mouse's I do "the squawk".

"KARGHH KARGHHHHH!"

Whenever me and Mouse need each other we've got a noise that we use. It sounds like a jungle bird and you can hear it from miles away. Mouse taught me how to do it and said, "Right, Archie, first rule of the squawk: do not teach anyone else the squawk. OK?"

"Why?" I asked.

"It's our call. When you hear it, you'll know it's me and when I hear it, I know it's you. When you hear the squawk you always answer – that's the second rule. Deal?"

"Deal."

And so, every morning outside her house, I do the squawk and she knows I'm outside. Once her neighbour popped his head out of the top window and shouted, "Can you stop making that ruddy noise every ruddy morning?" We shouted, "Sorry!" and then ran off in a fit of giggles. So now I only do a quiet version of the squawk in the mornings. I save the full version for when I *really* need her.

She skips out of her door and her mum and dad are behind her, waving her off.

"Morning, Archie!" Zoe shouts. "What on earth happened to your head?"

"I just came off my bike. I'm OK, but I'm really sorry, your dish broke."

"Don't be daft, it's only a dish. Are you sure you're OK? It looks like a pretty nasty bruise."

"Yeah, I'm fine!"

"Look after him today, Jasmin," Zoe calls after us.

"I will!" Mouse shouts and we head up the street.

Mouse's real name is Jasmin, but she hates it. She tried to get everyone at school to call her Minnie instead, but it went a bit wrong when Bella and Bea started calling her Minnie Mouse. Then everyone joined in and the Mouse bit stuck. She says she prefers it to Jasmin, so she's been Mouse ever since. It kind of suits her because she's really small – the second smallest in the year – but she is super strong and fast. I think she's about the toughest person I know.

I've known Mouse since we were at playgroup together. There are pictures of us with muddy faces, wearing nappies and holding sticks in her garden. Apparently, we loved making magic potions when we were tiny. I remember one time we even tried to sell some of our "magic rose petal perfume" from a little table outside her house. The only person who bought any was her mum, who gave us ten pence each and then pretended to dab it on her wrists. Mouse used to come round to our house too, when Dad lived with us. When we were like a normal family. Mum doesn't like having people in the house any more, so I just go to Mouse's now.

As we're walking up the hill to school, she says, "What's in your hair, Archie?" and I feel a crusty hard bit of hair above my ear.

"Shepherd's pie," I say. "I totally forgot to wash it out."

"You look like a right mess. How did you come off your bike?"

I start telling her about the slow motion and everything going black, and just as I'm getting to the best bit, the bit where I see Lucas Bailey, the wind blows, and leaves start swirling around our feet. We duck into the bus stop and I tell her everything.

She's silent for a while and looks a bit worried, and then the worry turns to anger.

"I spent all Sunday night studying for that maths test and then you cancelled it with a wish? Thanks a lot, Archie Crumb!"

"Sorry," I mumble.

Mouse bursts out laughing and I realize that she's not really angry, she's just pretending. Mouse is a pretty good actress so it's hard to know when she's messing about.

"You don't honestly think that *you* cancelled school, do you?" she says.

"But everything I wished for happened! The pizza, the Xbox, everything!"

Mouse starts pacing up and down in the bus shelter. She's in lawyer mode now. Mouse is obsessed with courtroom dramas; she watches them all the time.

"In your opening statement to the court, Mr Crumb, you asserted that your neighbour left the box for you the day *before* you made the wish – is that correct?"

"Yeah?"

"So the Xbox must have already been in it. Would you agree?"

"I guess."

Mouse pauses, as though she knows she has just

revealed the evidence that will win her case.

"Then how, Archie Crumb, if the Xbox arrived *before* the wish had even been made, could this be anything other than a crazy coincidence?"

"But the pizza? And school being cancelled?"

Mouse stops pacing. "Boilers break all the time, and it's not unheard of for a pizza to get delivered to the wrong house, is it?"

My shoulders slump.

"So you don't think it's real?" I ask, deflated.

She snaps out of lawyer mode and sits on the bench next to me.

"I'm not saying that it's *definitely* not real, but I do think that you will never really know for sure ... unless you wish for something truly impossible."

"Like what?"

"Well, that's up to you. Think of something that you really want. Something IMPOSSIBLE."

I think for a while. The big things I want feel sharp-edged and complicated: for Dad to love me and for Mum to get better. "What would *you* wish for?" I ask in the end.

"Gender equality. If I couldn't have that, then a pinball machine in my bedroom. But it doesn't matter what *I* would wish for, does it. You have got to figure out what YOU want. How about we meet after school and make a plan. Deal?"

"Deal." I smile.

"And absolutely no more wishing until then, OK?" I nod and she adds, "You might want to go and wash the mashed potato out of your hair too – before the B-B Gang see the state of you!" I laugh and pick a dried piece of carrot from my fringe and we head off to our separate classrooms.

"I could wish for Bella and Bea to be turned into pigs?!" I call after her. "Now that would make me **very** happy!"

CHAPTER SIX

**Pressure is something you feel when you
lack faith in yourself. —Lucas Bailey**

**Pressure is something I feel when I need to
fart in class. —Archie Crumb**

In English, Mrs Mather is talking about subordinate clauses. I stare at a page of questions that I will never know the answers to and drift off into Archie Land. I imagine Lucas Bailey at my age – sitting at this very desk, doing keepie-uppies in the playground at lunch. Living down the street in a tiny house with his brothers and sisters when he was spotted and started playing in the youth squad at Rovers. He must have wished so hard to win the Premiership and the Euros and the World Cup and every single one of his wishes came true. So maybe it is possible. Maybe, if I just wish for the right things, I can change my whole life...

"Archie Crumb, have you been listening to a single word I've said?"

I look up and Miss Mather is staring at me.

"Yes, miss," I say quickly.

"In that case, please tell the class your thoughts."

"No, miss," I say, even quicker. "Sorry, miss."

The whole class starts giggling and I hear Bella saying, "Yes, miss. No, miss. Three bags full, miss," in a squeaky voice behind me.

The rest of the day takes for ever and I'm desperate for it to end so I can talk to Mouse. At lunchtime Dan Dore asks if I want to play football. No one ever asks me to play, so that's nice. He's the only one who ever passes it to me, but when I score an own goal, even he stops. I guess you can only be so nice.

I can't wish for everyone to be kinder, but I could wish to be massive and scary and then everyone would *have* to be kinder to me. Although Frank Humpty, who is the biggest boy in school and is nearly as tall as Mr Fell, walks with a hunch like he wants to vanish and everyone calls him "Humpty Dumpty". I decide I don't fancy that much.

When the bell finally goes at the end of the day I

head out as quick as I can to the gate to meet Mouse.

"Let's go, magic man!" she says, and we head off down the hill. We get to the bus shelter and sit on the cold graffitied bench. There is nothing and nobody around, apart from a crisp packet blowing along the pavement and some boarded-up shops. I can hear a dog barking in the distance. It really doesn't look or sound like the kind of place where wishes can come true.

Mouse turns to me. "Right, I've got a plan. Let's forget about the wishes for now, just tell me some things you love."

"Like what?"

"Anything. Stuff that makes you happy."

I sit and watch the crisp packet blowing around, trying to remember times when I felt happy.

"Getting more football stickers?" I say.

"Good," she says, writing it down on a scrap of paper. "What else?"

"Playing with Scadge?"

"Perfect. Keep going."

"Obviously, I like watching the footy and hanging out with you, but I'm not sure what all this has got to do with wishing."

"Well, you have got to figure out who you are and

what you want to have any idea of what you should wish for, don't you?"

"I guess so."

"It's like my mum says: 'The universe can't give you what you want unless you know what you are asking for.'"

"I guess. . ." I say.

I start thinking about what I really want. What would make me happy. Then the thoughts start coming to me. Faster and faster.

I want a big family, who love each other and make each other laugh so hard that they cry.

I want to live in a big warm house and have friends over all the time, because I'm the most popular boy in school.

I want Nerf gun wars in the huge garden and a trampoline in the floor, a cinema and a ball pit.

I want to always have fizzy pop in the cupboard and Coco Pops on demand.

I want busy Christmases together where we play games with stickers on our heads and tins of chocolates that are so full you can't feel the bottom. I want there to be people smiling in a kitchen full of tasty smells every time I open the door after school. I want them to ask me how my day was and really want to know the answer. I want to have hundreds of cousins and uncles and aunties who all remember my birthday and send me cards every year. I want pets and bouncy castles and balloons and parties and music.

I want everything that I haven't got, but I can't say any of this out loud. Not to Mouse, not to anyone, because it's too much. I want too much and I don't even know where to start.

Mouse is looking at me hard, like she understands.

"How about we start small," she says gently. "See if we can prove whether this is even real. Let's say you wish for some football stickers. What's the craziest, most unlikely amount of football stickers you could get?"

"I could find a packet on my way home?" I suggest brightly.

"Bigger than that, Archie!!"

"I find *nine* packets on my way home!"

"BIGGER!" she shouts.

"One hundred and nine packets?!" I ask.

"More like it, but I'm thinking *truly* impossible."

I think for a minute. "I saw a competition once to win the biggest football sticker collection in the world, can you imagine that?"

"Did you enter it?"

"No," I say. "I didn't have enough money for the stamp."

I'd excitedly filled in the form and then asked Mum for 70p.

"Leave me alone, Archie," she'd groaned from under her duvet. "Always asking me for things. You have no idea how hard it is for me." I knew then that I needed to get out quickly and that my dream of having the biggest sticker collection ever was over.

She always says that. That I have "no idea" and that I "don't understand". She has no idea either and doesn't understand what it's like for me. I always want to say that back to her, but I never dare. She would go off on one talking about her "symptoms" and then shouting or crying – or probably both. I guess no one can really ever understand what it's like for someone else, can they?

"Well, that's it, Archie Crumb," Mouse says, pulling my attention back to the bus stop. "You have found your wish. To have the biggest football sticker collection in the world. Wish for that and we'll know whether Magic Lucas and his wishes are real."

I hesitate. It seems like a ridiculous thing to wish for. Mouse leans forward.

"If you don't wish for it, then it definitely can't

come true, can it?"

I nod and close my eyes. I imagine myself in front of a HUGE pile of stickers. Then I whisper in a tiny voice, "I wish I had the biggest sticker collection in the world."

"Louder," whispers Mouse.

"I wish I had the biggest sticker collection in the world," I repeat a little louder, the picture getting stronger in my mind.

"Louder!" she says again. "You have to believe in it, Archie. Say it like you really want it."

"I WISH I HAD THE BIGGEST STICKER COLLECTION IN THE WORLD!" I shout at the top of my voice, and in the same moment the wind blows hard and sends the empty crisp packet flying into my face. When I bat it off and look over the road, I can see Bella and Bea laughing and pointing at me.

"I WISH, I WISH," they start chanting in shrill sing-song voices. "I WISH I WASN'T ARCHIE CRUMB."

CHAPTER SEVEN

Nothing and no one is perfect, that's why pencils come with a rubber on the end.
–Lucas Bailey

My pencils came in a Tesco value pack – they don't have a rubber on the end.
–Archie Crumb

I scan the road the whole way home, searching for anything unusual, and find – absolutely nothing. No giant sticker collection. No medium-sized sticker collection. Nothing. Not even a single sticker.

Back home, I take a Lucas double out and smile. "I guess the Xbox was just a coincidence," I tell him. "Oh well. It was fun while it lasted – feeling like anything was possible. Thanks for trying, Lucas – you're still my favourite."

I really LOVE collecting stickers. Dad started buying them for me years ago, but he doesn't bother any more. Some weekends he gives me a pound and says, "Get yourself a chocolate bar or something, Arch." Every time he gives me any money, I use it to buy stickers. I ask for stickers for every birthday and Christmas too. I have filled four books and have the tenth biggest collection in school. The kids who have bigger collections aren't even that bothered. They got bought all the stickers in one go and filled up their books straight away, then got bored. Not like me – I care about every single sticker, and when I get one that I need, I carefully cross it off my list and then use my best sticking technique, the technique that I have perfected, which leaves me with no bubbles, wrinkles or gaps. I have even written a guide to good sticking in case I ever forget or have to pass on my collection to someone else:

ARCHIE CRUMB'S GUIDE
TO GOOD STICKING

1. **Make sure the page is clear of crumbs, dust and bits.** I once had a terrible time

trying to unstick Idrissa Gueye's face and remove a tiny crumb of toast that was making his eye bulge.

2. **Line up the top two corners and peel the backing away from those two corners only.** This is the most important bit. Any wonkiness here cannot be corrected later – see page 112 of book 1 for proof of how wonky a sticker can be. Thank goodness I have learned since then.

3. **Place sticker with tension at both sides and confidently press down.** Confidence is key here. Any faffing about and that's where creases happen. Don't let the voice in your head tell you that this is not going to be the best stick you have ever done.

4. **Slowly remove backing whilst pressing sticker towards you, maintaining an even pressure throughout.** Too fast = bubbles. Too slow = creasing.

5. **Firmly smooth out the sticker and put backing in bin.** Or if you are like me and save the backs too, place in the Backs Pile, which is located next to the Wrappers Pile.

Once I proudly showed this to Mouse, and she called me "bonkers".

"It's important!" I said.

"Don't worry, if I ever have to stick any of your stickers I will keep to the rules. I will learn them by heart and repeat them daily. I will blow the rules up and stick a poster of them on my wall!"

"Well, there is no need for that," I said, but secretly I thought that this all sounded great.

I'm dragged back to reality by a loud knock at the door. I run downstairs and feel a familiar shiver down my spine. I shake it off and open the door.

There's a white lorry parked up on the pavement outside. Two men are unloading huge heavy-looking boxes on to a trolley thing. When they see me the tall man in a woolly hat says, "Are you Archie Crumb?"

"Yeah," I say.

"Where do you want them? Shall we stack 'em up by the door?"

"What's in them?" I ask.

"Dunno, little man, we just deliver stuff." I watch as the men bring out box after box and stack them in eight towering piles.

"Hang on a minute!" I say as they just keep on coming. "There must be a mistake!"

"Only sixteen more to come, fella," the shorter hatless man pants as he heaves the box he's holding on to the top of a pile. I'm starting to panic. The boxes nearly cover the whole of the front of the house now. *Mum will not like this*, I think – then I wonder whether she'll even notice. When they are finally finished, the tall man says:

"Can you sign this, please?"

He passes me a clipboard and a pen. I love signing things. I do my best signature; I've been practising it for years.

I do a huge *A* and draw a smiley face inside and then the *C* wraps right around the outside and circles the *Archie*.

When I finish, he hands me an envelope and says, "Righty ho. Good luck getting them all inside." He jumps back in his van before I can ask anything else.

After watching the lorry drive away, I turn and look at the wall of boxes in front of me. I try to squeeze behind them to get to the front door but there's no room and I end up wedging myself between two of the towers. I try to lift one but it's far too high and heavy. I don't want to be crushed by a tower of boxes.

That's when I remember the bus shelter and my wish. I can feel the excitement inside me building up. Suddenly, I have to open the box and find out whether it's true.

I rip open the top of one of the boxes. I can't quite crane my head to see inside. I raise my hand and, when I stand on my tiptoes, I can just reach it down into the box. I move my hand around and feel all of the shiny wrappers between my fingers.

"It came true!" I squeak to myself. "It actually came true! It's stickers. They are all full to the brim with stickers!"

Two wishes have come true, and that means I have seven wishes left!

I start doing a little dance amongst all the boxes. I can feel bolts of excitement like electricity shooting through my body and my brain, making me dance and shuffle faster and faster.

My wishes have been granted.

My wishes have been granted.

My wishes have been granted.

I feel so happy. Everything is now possible. I could do ANYTHING. I could fly to the moon or swim with dolphins, I could lie in a chocolate fountain or meet the queen, I could be a YouTube star or an

Olympic swimmer, I could beat everyone in the next maths test and be the top of the class. My life is about to get a whole lot better – but first I had better figure out a way to get these boxes inside.

I try to move the boxes but I don't get very far – who knew that stickers could be so heavy? My arms are killing me and I've managed to move one box five centimetres. Also, I really need a wee and the boxes are blocking the front door.

I give up and sit on the kerb.

A man is walking a little dog down the road and I wonder if he can help. But as I stand up and walk towards him, he picks up his little dog and says, "No, thank you." Then he hurries away.

That's a weird thing to say when you don't even know what I was going to ask, I think. Some people seem terrified of everything – even of a little kid asking for help.

I'm *desperate* for a wee now and start hopping from foot to foot. I'm not sure how this helps but it does. I jiggle my way round to the back of the house and see if I can call Mum to come and help. I know that the chances of her hearing me from her bed are slim, but it's worth a try.

Through the passage and round the back,

underneath her bedroom window, I start shouting in a loud whisper, "Mum, Mum, MUM!" The whisper turns into a bellow. I'm hopping up and down, desperately trying not to wee my pants.

"Are you all right, Archie?" comes a voice from a few windows up. It's Rosemary at number twelve. She looks at my jiggling and adds, "Do you need to use my loo?"

"Yes, please!" I say, and dash over.

She lets me in and I sprint past her little brown dog, who's yapping at me and spinning in circles.

"Ignore Sir Lancelot," Rosemary says. "He's all noise. First door on the left, sweetheart."

After I've been to the toilet – which is a massive relief – and washed my hands, I start to feel a bit embarrassed. Rosemary's house is really nice and calm. It smells like flowers and there are little pictures all over the walls. It doesn't feel like the sort of house you should sprint into, yelling for the toilet.

When I come out, Rosemary is standing in the kitchen with Sir Lancelot in her arms, and her son, James, is sitting at the kitchen table. He's the one who gave me the Xbox. The last time I saw him he was a taller, spottier version of me, but now he looks old enough to be my dad.

"James is visiting from uni," Rosemary says. "Do you want some juice?"

"No, thanks, I'd better go. Thanks for letting me use your loo." Then I add, "And thanks for the box of stuff. I loved it. Especially the Xbox."

"Do you like FIFA?" James says. "I was obsessed when I first got it."

"Yeah. I'm a bit rubbish though."

He laughs and flicks his hair off his face. His clothes are all black and baggy and his hair falls straight back over his eyes. I wonder if I could beat him at FIFA; he probably couldn't even see the screen. As if he can read my mind, he says: "If you ever want a game I can pop over and play – relive my youth."

Looking at him standing there like a baggy, hairy giant in the kitchen gives me an idea.

"Actually, I don't suppose you could do me a big favour and come over now? I've got a load of boxes blocking the front door. I need a hand getting them inside."

Rosemary frowns. "Is that why you were shouting, love? Is your mum not in?"

"She must have music on or something," I lie.

Rosemary nods. "You'll give him a hand, won't you, love?" she says to James.

"Yeah, no worries," James says, and pulls his shoes on. "Always happy to help a fellow FIFA fan."

"What's in these boxes anyway?" he asks, dragging box number ten away from the front door. "They're so heavy!"

"Football stickers," I say.

"You're joking? I used to love football stickers. Why have you got this many?!"

"Don't ask. I don't really understand it myself," I say. "Take as many as you like!"

He laughs and I open the front door.

"Right," he says. "Let's get this lot inside then."

That's when I realize that this might be a bad idea. My cleaning regime has been non-existent recently, so the house is pretty bad. And I know that Mum doesn't like it when people come over, so I just shrug and say, "You know what, it's fine actually, I'll just bring in as many packets as I can at a time."

"You'll be here all night! Don't be daft."

He begins carrying the boxes in one by one. I hurry in and quickly shut the door to the kitchen so that he can't see how much stuff is piled up on the sides. It doesn't smell too good either but there's nothing I can do about that. Maybe I should wish for the house to smell better.

The boxes start piling up on every surface. Wobbly piles on the sofa and chairs, and high up in front of the little broken gas fire. There are boxes stacked up to the ceiling in front of the window, blocking out the light. There are boxes filling the entire room, until I can't see any of the walls any more. The whole room is boxes.

When the last one is squeezed in, I try to say thanks in a really casual way, but I can see him looking around the room. His face is worried.

"Where's your mum, Archie?" he says quietly.

"Ah, she's just up in bed. She's got a cold."

"I thought you said she was listening to music?"

"Yes. Both," I say. "Anyway I'd better go and check on her. You should go. You don't want to catch anything, do you?"

"How long has she been ill for?"

"Just a couple of days," I say as I squeeze past him and open the door. "Thanks so much for helping," and I lead him out of the door, closing it quickly behind him.

Then I turn around to look at the boxes and sit down on the floor. I have no idea what I'm going to do with them all.

I open the first box and frown. I'm expecting to see a sea of red shiny packets with thousands of inspirational quotes staring back up at me, telling me to *Dream Big!* and *Be the Change I Want to See.*

But instead, there is a huge box full of pastel colours. Pinks and blues and shapes and patterns all mixed in together. I take out a handful and look through them and my heart sinks.

These are not what I wished for! There are Disney stickers and animal stickers, stickers with emojis on. Packet after packet and sheet after sheet of completely useless stickers. I look in another box and find the same thing, and then another. I eventually find a box that is mainly football stickers – more football stickers than I have ever seen in my lifetime – but still I'm surrounded by Donald Duck and princesses.

I pick up the phone and call Mouse.

When she finally stops laughing at the idea of me being completely overwhelmed by babyish stickers, she pauses and then says, "In the bus stop, Archie, what EXACTLY did you wish for?"

"The biggest sticker collection in the—" I stop halfway through, realizing what I've done.

"You just asked for stickers? Not *football* stickers?"

"Oh no!"

When she stops laughing for the second time, I tell her that I'd better go. "I need to get these stickers into my room before my mum sees them!"

Of course the wish can't see inside my brain and know exactly what I mean. I need to be more careful from now on. Only seven more wishes to go. I can't make any more silly mistakes.

After two hours I have only emptied three boxes and my room is already piled high with stickers. I get into a system: I fill two rucksacks and put one on my front and one on my back, and then fill up two Tesco bags and carry them all upstairs. Mum won't be happy if she comes down and finds the living room full of stickers, not that she ever goes in there, especially since the telly is still in my room. I wonder how long it would take until she noticed that the room was full of boxes. Probably months.

After my seventh trip up the stairs, I decide to take a break and tidy up the kitchen a bit. Having James in the house made me realize I need to look after things a bit better. I don't want anyone to think that something's wrong. Mum tells me not to tell anyone about how much time she spends in bed.

"People start sticking their nose in, Archie, but we're OK, aren't we?"

"Yeah, I guess," I say.

"Promise you won't tell anyone."

She looks really serious when she says it, scared. It feels important. That's why I try to hide Mum's illness from everyone. Even Mouse doesn't know how poorly she is.

I wash up the bowls first. We only have three bowls and so if I don't wash them right away I have to start eating things straight out of the tin – which is what I've been doing.

I count eight empty spaghetti hoop tins, three tomato soup tins and four beans-with-sausage tins. As I put them in the bin, I make a promise to myself to wash the bowls straight away when I am done with them and to stop eating out of tins. We did a thing about healthy eating at school last week and Kiran and Martha said they cook fancy meals like rice with vegetables and fish pie with broccoli and green beans. I lied about what I eat and I definitely didn't mention the eating straight from the tin phase. Afterwards, when I was doing the online shop, I ordered some broccoli, but then when I added cheese slices it went over £40 so I had to take out the broccoli – I love cheese slices. I melt them on to my hot spaghetti hoops – delicious!

When the kitchen looks a bit better, I finish taking the stickers up to my room. Every surface is covered. It looks like a sticker volcano has erupted in my bedroom. As I sit on the bed and feel the packets of football stickers in my hand, I realize that I am not even interested in opening them. There are just too many. Maybe this is what it's like for the kids who get given loads all at once and fill up a book in one day. There's no joy in it if you already know you have enough.

I find my wish list and fill in number two:

ARCHIE CRUMB'S WISH LIST

1. XBOX & PIZZA
2. THE BIGGEST STICKER COLLECTION IN THE WORLD
3.
4.
5.
6.
7.
8.
9.

I decide that I'll take loads of the stickers into school and sell them. Maybe I can earn enough to add some broccoli to the next shop. Mouse can help. She's the best saleswoman ever and she'll have a successful sticker stall up in no time.

Last summer, she came up with an idea to sell homemade dog biscuits at the end of the road. She made people laugh at the story of how her dog Eric wouldn't eat and how every day she tried something new until one day when they had run out of hope she baked some peanut butter treats and Eric stole them off the kitchen side and ate the whole lot. After people had stopped saying, "Ahh, how lovely," and laughing at all of her jokes, it was pretty clear that they were going to buy some treats, even if they had no dog. I just sat at the table and watched in awe.

I'm excited about having a sticker stall and earning some money. If I can earn loads then maybe that means I don't need to waste a wish on finding a big pile of cash. As I sit, surrounded by my stickers, I think about what I should wish for next.

The sticker wish just wasn't clear enough. I have to be more specific. Lucas was right: I need to be clever about this. I'm not going to rush into anything. This is too important.

CHAPTER EIGHT

The harder you work, the luckier you become. —Lucas Bailey

What about the time when Bella won the class raffle? The only thing she works hard at is being horrible. —Archie Crumb

I sleep way past my alarm in the morning and rush out without having breakfast or saying bye to Mum. On my way out of the door, I see the envelope that the lorry driver gave me lying on the pavement. I must have dropped it when I was trying to move all of the boxes. It's a bit soggy but I pick it up, shove it in my bag and run to school.

I go straight past Mouse's without even bothering

to do the squawk – I'm so late she'll have gone ahead.

I sneak in to assembly and on to the edge of a row as Mrs Jain, the headteacher, is giving a talk.

"If you can imagine how someone else might feel, then you can make the right choices," she is saying. "That's what empathy is all about."

I glance down the row. Jayden Thomas is poking Dan Dore in the sides, making Dan flinch every time his fingers dig in. The B-Bs are laughing hysterically. I wonder if they have any idea what empathy even is. I'm half-tempted to make a wish right there and then, a wish to get rid of the B-B Gang so that I never have to look at their mean faces again. But then I hear Mrs Jain saying:

"Sometimes you may not understand someone else, but there is always a story there. Let's try and find out about each other's stories. Today I challenge you to learn something new about someone in your class. Let's build Valleybrook Primary into a school filled with empathy." She waits for a moment, as if she's expecting us to start clapping and cheering. No one does.

When she realizes that we aren't all going to erupt into spontaneous applause, she sighs and says, "OK, everyone, quietly back to class, please."

On our way to our classrooms, Mouse catches me up.

"Where were you?" she says, walking along the corridor with me.

"I slept in!" I whisper. "It's all the excitement – I'm exhausted! You should see my bedroom, it's insane. I've never seen so many stickers in my life. These wishes are TOTALLY real, Mouse."

Mouse is clearly thinking hard because her eyebrows are scrunched down and her face is scrunched up. "There must be a logical explanation! What did the delivery people say? Did they tell you where the stickers had come from?"

"No, nothing," I say. Then I remember the envelope from this morning and rummage through my bag.

"They did give me this, though," I say, pulling it out. "I didn't open it."

"Why not?!"

"I needed a wee – I got distracted."

"Oh, Archie – give it here," she says. She grabs the envelope and rips it open. "Just as I thought. A perfectly non-magical explanation!"

I look at her, confused.

"You won the competition!"

"What competition?!"

"The one you told me about."

"But I didn't *enter* the competition!"

"You must have!" she says, shoving the letter under my eyes.

CONGRATULATIONS, ARCHIE CRUMB!!
 You are now officially the proud new owner
 of the world's largest sticker collection!!
 Enjoy your prize!

"But – but I never sent the form – and anyway the competition was for *football* stickers."

"Are you sure?"

I try and remember. "I don't know," I say at last. "It was so long ago. But I **definitely** didn't post it."

"Maybe your mum posted it?"

"No, she never leaves the house!" I say. Then I worry I've said too much, but Mouse doesn't seem to notice and carries on.

"Well, someone must have. You probably just forgot, Archie."

I nod, but I know that I *did not* post that form. As we reach my classroom door and Mouse keeps going towards hers, she says, "There is always an explanation for things." Then she adds, "Archie, if you really need more proof that this is all just a bizarre coincidence, then you have to go even further."

Mrs Mather's voice comes out of the classroom. "Enough chatting! Sit down, everyone, please; independent reading books out."

"Go!" says Mouse, and I quickly dash into the classroom, slink into my seat and pretend to stare at my book. But for the rest of the morning, and all through lunch and art that afternoon, I'm just thinking about magical wishes and my mountain of stickers.

When we're finally out of school and sitting at the bus stop, I say to Mouse, "I thought we could sell the stickers."

She gets excited right away. "Yes! Now that is good thinking, Archie. Only I'm not doing it at school! Mrs Turner caught me taking bets on the Euros last year and called my parents, so if she catches me setting up a sticker-selling shop I'll be in big trouble. We'll have to do it somewhere else."

"How about in here?!" I ask, gesturing to the shelter. It's covered in graffiti and chewing gum, but Mouse nods enthusiastically.

"A sticker stop – I like it." She takes out a notebook and starts scribbling. "We need to sort them all out into categories first, so that you can give people what they want. Like a proper shop. Shall I come over and help you sort?"

"Erm, no, it's OK, I'll do it," I say quickly. "It'll be boring."

Mouse nods again. She knows not to ask twice.

"OK, well, you sort them out and I'll make a sign..." She raises her arms, imagining a huge sign on the back of the bus shelter. "Mouse and Crumb's Magic Sticker Stop Emporium."

"Crumb and Mouse, not Mouse and Crumb!! Whose wishes are these, remember?!" I laugh.

I stop laughing a second later, though, because I can see the B-Bs on the other side of the road, smirking and pointing at us. Then comes the tinkling sound of an ice cream van over the hill.

"Ooh, I'm **so** hot, I would love an ice cream!" Mouse says, looking in her pocket for money.

"Me too," I sigh, knowing that there's no point looking in my pockets.

"Come on," she shouts, and she dashes over the road to where the van's parking up.

I follow.

"I've only got enough for one," Mouse says, looking through her coins. "We can share it."

There's a nasty laugh behind us and I freeze. Bella and Bea have joined the queue.

"Poor Archie," says Bella, in a horrible, fake-sympathetic voice. "Haven't you got any money for an ice cream? It's no wonder, if your mum is too **lazy** to even turn up for work."

"Leave him alone!" Mouse says with a scowl.

"It's all right, Mouse. You get one. I don't really want one anyway," I say.

"Are you OK?" she whispers.

"Yeah, I'm used to them." I try to make a joke out of it. "I wish I had my own ice cream van. I would eat until I was sick and NEVER serve those two if I did, that's for sure!"

"Imagine us in our own van! Mouse and Crumb's Ices. That would be so cool."

I close my eyes and imagine me and Mouse looking out of the little glass hatch holding the biggest ice creams in the world.

The wind blows and a tingle runs down my spine. A phone starts ringing from inside the van and my eyes pop open – what have I just done?!

We get to the front of the queue as the ice cream

man finishes serving the boy in front of us. He's talking on the phone. There are loads of people behind us and the queue is getting longer and longer.

"Sorry, guys. Just a minute, yeah?" the man in the van says to us, putting his hand over his phone.

"Did you feel that gust of wind?" I whisper to Mouse.

"No. Why?"

"I think I might have done something," I say. "Did – did I just wish for an ice cream van?"

Before Mouse can answer, the man appears back at the hatch. His face looks pale and he is taking his apron off as quickly as he can.

"You're going to have to serve yourselves," he says, putting a set of keys in my hand. You're in charge. Serve everyone else in the queue – apart from those two." I see that he's pointing towards Bella and Bea, who gasp in shock. "Then you can eat as much ice cream as you like. OK?" he says.

He dashes out of the back door of the van and calls over his shoulder, "I'll be back later! Just look after it, OK? It's your ice cream van until I get back!" We watch him sprinting down the road.

The B-Bs start shuffling and tutting. A woman

further back laughs kindly and says, "You better get in and start serving or you'll be here all night!"

No one seems to be finding this whole thing as weird as they should be. They're behaving as if it's completely normal for someone to entrust an eleven-year-old with an ice cream van.

"I've always wanted to look inside one!" Mouse says. "Come on!"

We scramble inside. I can see the lever and the nozzle where the ice cream comes out. There are sprinkles and sauces and a box of Flakes next to a fridge which is full of lollies. Everything you can imagine. Fabs, Twisters, Screwballs, Rockets, EVERYTHING.

I turn to Mouse, who's looking at the tubs of chopped nuts and hundreds and thousands, and she looks back at me in amazement.

"OK, I'm starting to enjoy these wishes, Archie."

"I didn't even mean to wish for this one!" I grin.

"Well, there's no point wasting it, is there?" she says, shoving a Flake into her mouth and turning to the hatch and the line of customers.

We figure out how to make the nozzle work and pop our heads out of the window. Bella and Bea are still there.

"Two double 99s with sauce and sprinkles," demands Bella, slamming her money down on the counter.

"I'm afraid I can't serve you," I say, smiling down at them as sweetly as I can. I'm feeling more powerful than I have ever felt around the stupid B-Bs. "You heard what the man said. So did everyone else in the queue. Now could you please step aside so that I can serve these polite people who have been waiting so patiently?"

"But – but – this isn't fair!" cries Bella.

The woman next in line pushes them to one side. "Excuse me, girls!" she says, then adds, "Maybe next time you'll think twice about being so mean. We all heard what you were saying to this lad. You don't deserve any ice cream!" She turns to me. "Two Twisters, please."

"Fine," snarls Bella. "The ice cream here is rubbish anyway!"

I ignore her and serve the woman. Out of the corner of my eye I can see Bella stomping and shouting, and Bea looking like she might pop with fury, but I just carry on taking people's orders. It feels so good! Eventually they storm off and Mouse and I high-five.

It's actually really hard work, trying to remember the orders, give the right change and keep smiling! After a couple of pretty disastrous wobbly ice creams, we get into a good rhythm where I squirt from the nozzle, Mouse adds the toppings and sauces and I take the money. They still don't look like the best ice creams in the world, but we're pretty generous with the sauce and so no one complains.

When the last teenager gets to the hatch and we give him a 99 he says, "I wish I worked in an ice cream van. You're so lucky!"

When everyone's gone we close up the hatch and flop down on the little bench.

"I tell you what, I could do with some ice cream!" Mouse says as she lies underneath the nozzle with her mouth wide open.

"A double, please, Mr Crumb, with extra sauce and sprinkles."

"Certainly, madam," I say, pushing the nozzle down and laughing as I squirt whippy ice cream all over her face. She squeals but can't move as the ice cream threatens to slide off on to the floor.

"Sprinkles, madam?" I ask, and she giggles from underneath her faceful and I add sprinkles and sauces all over her face, to the sound of ice-creamy squealing.

"Anything else, madam?" I say, laughing hard now, and Mouse takes a handful of ice cream from her nose and plunges it straight into my face.

An ice cream fight, a Fab, a Twister and a Feast later, we clean up the mess and we're sitting with two of the biggest 99s you've ever seen, covered in every single thing you can imagine: strawberry sauce, chocolate sprinkles, three Flakes in each and a bubble gum on top.

"If you've got an ice cream van just think about what else you could have!" Mouse says as we both sit there slurping, feeling happy, tired and sick, imagining what else we could wish for. Mouse's phone beeps and she looks at it.

"Archie, I've got to go home. Mum's doing her nut, wondering where I am."

"Don't worry, I'll stay here," I say. My mum won't have even noticed that I'm not home.

When she's gone, it starts to get dark outside and the autumn air feels suddenly colder. The van doesn't feel quite as cosy as it did before. I put the keys into the ignition to see if I can turn the radio on, but the jingle suddenly starts ringing out from the van. It's loud and makes me jump.

In the dusky evening light, the sound of the chime

seems creepy, and I turn the key quickly to switch it off. I'm not sure how long I should wait. I don't want to leave the van with the keys in it, but I can't stay here all night. I'm feeling pretty sick after all the chocolate sauce, so I lie down in the back and put my coat over me to keep me warm.

I must have dozed off. I dream about climbing a mountain made of ice cream with Lucas Bailey, our feet sinking in deep with every step. When we get to the top we start celebrating but then I fall. I can see my mum at the bottom, but she's not looking at me and doesn't notice that I'm falling...

I jolt awake and see the ice cream man leaning over me, gently shaking my shoulders. He looks tired and very happy.

"You stayed!" he says.

"Yeah," I say, rubbing my eyes. "I didn't want to leave the keys." I look out of the hatch and see that it's now completely dark outside.

"Well, little man, I can't thank you enough. I'm so sorry for leaving you like that. My wife's waters broke and she thought that she wasn't going to make it to the hospital in time to get the baby out. We only live round the corner, so I just had to run!"

"Is she OK?" I ask.

"Yes. She's cuddling our baby boy at the hospital right now."

"Congratulations," I say. I know that's what adults say to each other when they have babies.

"How was being an ice cream man for the afternoon?!"

"Fun!" I say, and then I add, "It did get a bit messy and we ate quite a lot of ice cream!"

"I should hope you did! You can have free ice cream for the rest of your life! What's your name?"

"Archie Crumb," I say, and then my tummy gurgles and I add, "I'm not sure I could eat another ice cream in my life!"

"Ha! That happens. I don't think I've had one for years! I'm Martin," he says as I get my coat on. "Archie – that's a nice name. We thought the baby was going to be a girl, so we don't have any boy names ready. Baby Archie. I like it! How would you feel about having a namesake?"

"That would be pretty cool!" I say.

"Now, shall I drop you home? I can apologize to your parents for keeping you out!"

"No, thank you, it's not far," I say, and step out into the dark night, the ice cream man waving me off as I go.

If I hadn't made that wish, baby Archie wouldn't be named after me. Maybe it wasn't because of the wish at all though. Maybe it was because I stayed in the van and didn't just leave it. Maybe it's not **just** the wishing that makes good things happen. I feel in my pocket and get out Lucas.

"I could have stolen the van or given away all of the ice cream. Or if my mum was worried about where I was, I could have run home and left the van sitting empty. Then there would be no baby Archie, would there? It would have been a Tom or a Billy. So, it's not just the wishing, is it? It's what you do with the wish that really makes the difference."

I find myself smiling down at Lucas. And it might just be a trick of the light, but I'm sure I can see his eyes twinkling back up at me.

CHAPTER NINE

All the best decisions I have made have been on instinct. —Lucas Bailey

Is "instinct" something that smells bad? —Archie Crumb

Morning assembly again. I'm rubbing the sleep out of my eyes when Mrs Jain says, "Now, Mr Fell is here with some BIG news. Mr Fell, over to you."

A kid at the front says, "Fell over!" and everyone starts giggling.

Mr Fell was my teacher last year. At first, he seemed like he didn't really like kids very much, but when we got to know him, he was actually pretty funny. He just always sounds a bit sarcastic. Like once, when Bea was throwing her pen up and down instead of getting on with her work, Mr Fell said, "Wow, Bea, that's some skilful pen-throwing action you've got there. That'll serve you well in life. Almost as well as those fractions you should be doing."

Bea just mumbled and put her head down. I'd love to shut the B-Bs up like that, but I can never think of what to say in the moment. I go home and replay scenes again and again until I have the perfect line:

"Bella, if school was all about how mean you can be then you would get A stars."

Or:

"I wouldn't mind you stealing my pencil if I thought you were going to write something interesting with it."

Maybe now I won't need any of these lines. I remember their angry faces yesterday, as I sent them away from *my* ice cream van, and smile to myself.

"Thank you, Mrs Jain. Now, listen up, you lot," Mr Fell says, and I snap back to the assembly.

"Next month Valley Rovers are launching an inter-school football tournament for year five and six. There will be schools invited to play from across the country and they want us to take part – after all, we're Lucas Bailey's old school, aren't we?"

A couple of kids at the back start chanting, "Bailey,

Bailey, Bailey." Everyone loves Lucas Bailey so much that Mr Fell can't tell kids off for chanting his name – it's just part of living round here, like a law. You HAVE to love Lucas Bailey.

Mr Fell smiles and carries on. "So, with that in mind, we need to present the strongest team possible, to show that Valleybrook still has world-class sporting talent. The awards will be presented by none other than. . ." He does a drum roll on his knees and we all join in with our feet.

"That's right, Lucas Bailey himself!"

There's a ripple of excitement that goes around the hall and some of the kids whoop and cheer. My heart is beating fast. Lucas Bailey!

"I will be holding trials for the final team line-up after school next Wednesday. Anyone who wants to be in with a chance of going to the tournament needs to sign up after assembly on the sign-up sheet outside." My heart sinks. I will never make the team.

"Now, if you have never played before, don't let that hold you back. Lucas wants *everyone* to try out, whatever age or ability. There will be at least two spots in the final line-up for kids who have never been on the team. Right, that's it, now you can all get to lessons."

The hall erupts into instant chatter. I have to get on that team. To play at Valley Stadium and to meet Lucas again, to thank him for the wishes. I close my eyes tight and am just about to make my wish, but as I try to imagine myself on the Valley Stadium pitch I hear Bella's nasty voice chime out.

"What's that little weirdo doing? I think he's gone to sleep!" I feel a poke in my back and open my eyes to see Bella and Bea and a group of kids standing around me laughing. How dare they interrupt my wishing. They ruin everything. As they keep giggling and pointing at me and pretending to fall asleep, I feel my face getting hot.

"Ooh, look, he's wide awake now and he's getting angry. Watch out, everyone!" As I look at their horrible mean faces, I can feel my embarrassment turn to anger, but they just keep on laughing. Then I do it.

Staring right at Bella and Bea, I shout, "I wish you knew what it was like to be laughed at."

Then I close my eyes again and hear them howling and screeching, "Look! He's doing it again! He's asleep!"

I picture everyone laughing and pointing at Bella and Bea, and while the picture is strong in my head, I hear them chanting, "I WISH ... I WISH ... I WISH I WASN'T ARCHIE CRUMB!"

They keep chanting as they leave the hall, and I open my eyes and smile to myself.

After school, I meet Mouse and we head to the bus shelter. Before I can tell her about the B-B wish, she looks at me seriously.

"You're not thinking about using one of the wishes to get into the tournament, are you?"

"No...! Yes... Why, would that be so bad?"

"Yes, it would be so bad! Archie, the tournament is about finding the best players and it's not about cheating. It's about getting a place on the team because you deserve to be there, not because you can just take the easy route."

"OK, OK, I won't," I say, hesitating before I add, "You should definitely get in."

"I doubt it. I'm the only girl on the list and they don't like putting one girl on the team, in case I get barged by all the boys. Even though I'm twice as fast as most boys and more likely to go in for a tackle than all of them – it's stupid."

"Yeah, that must be so annoying," I sigh. "Imagine Lucas Bailey handing you a trophy. I wonder if he would recognize me, if I got to meet him. Do you think it was really him that night?"

"Who knows, Archie. It's really weird. I was thinking, though, and all of these brilliant things happening to you COULD still be coincidences."

"Are you serious?! I don't know about you but I still feel sick from all that ice cream that I WISHED FOR!"

"I'm just saying that it's not beyond possibility. Some bloke's wife having a baby is not exactly *abracadabra*, is it? The only way we will know for sure is if you wish for something TRULY impossible – something that *only* magic could create."

"Like what?"

"You're on your own with that, I've got to get home. Mum said if I don't clean out Flump by five p.m. she's taking her to a rescue centre for neglected gerbils."

"Do they even exist?" I ask as she starts heading off down the hill.

"I doubt it," she calls back over her shoulder. "But I don't want to risk finding out!"

When I get home the lights are on, and as I open the door, I see Mum in the kitchen. I can't stop an enormous, daft grin spreading across my face. I am *so happy* that she's out of bed. And then, immediately, I feel stupid and embarrassed. Like a little kid who runs out of school shouting, 'Mummy, Mummy, I missed you!'

I rearrange my face into a slightly cooler expression and go into the kitchen.

"Did you make tea?" I ask.

"Just some pasta pesto. I know you love the cheesy sauce best, but we're out of cheese. Good day?"

"Yeah, thanks." I look at her and she yawns, and I know that she's about to tell me that she needs to go to bed. I try desperately to think of something I can talk to her about, so that she'll stay.

Mum can be pretty great at listening sometimes. It's weird, like she can help me with my stuff but she's not so good with her own. Once the B-B Gang stuck chewing gum in my hair. I tried to get it out myself but it just got more and more stuck and in the end I had to ask her to cut it out. As she gently snipped around it, she asked me what had happened and listened when I told her about how the B-Bs are kind of mean to everyone, but really mean to me.

When I had finished telling her, she gave me a hug and said, "You know that I used to work for Bella's dad?"

I nodded. Of course I knew that. It was part of the reason we were in this mess.

"Well, he's not a nice man, Archie. He was horrible to me."

"Really?" I said.

"Really. I'm not surprised that Bella can be mean. He's a cruel man. Everyone gets it from somewhere. We pass these things on, Archie. It's terribly sad really. It doesn't make it OK what they're doing to you, it's no excuse – but it's always handy to know that everyone has their own stuff going on."

Maybe it's even more important that I teach Bella a lesson before it's too late and she becomes horrible for ever. But if Bella's a bully because of her dad, what does that mean for me? I don't want to end up like Mum, crying in bed. Now, every time I feel tired and don't want to get up in the morning, I panic that it might be the start of me becoming like her. That gets me up quick, I can tell you.

I don't want to become a liar like my dad either. It's impossible for me to tell a white lie now without feeling bad. Like when I told Mrs Mather that I had "lost" my homework sheet, I started worrying so much that I was turning into my dad that a week later I told her the truth – that I had accidentally used the sheet to make a paper aeroplane and then had thrown it into a puddle. She was pretty good about it and thanked me for being honest. So now I ALWAYS try to tell the truth *and* never sleep in the day. I think they are two pretty good personality traits. Maybe I should wish not to turn out like my parents? But Lucas said I can't wish to change anyone on the inside.

"Well, enjoy your tea, love," Mum says now, and goes towards the door.

"There's a football tournament happening at Valley Stadium!" I say quickly.

She stops and turns – it's working. "Ooh, very fancy. Are you going?"

I shrug. "I really want to but I don't think I'll make the team."

"Well, maybe you need a bit more practice. It should be in your blood – back in the day I was pretty good!" she says.

"I know! Do you remember that time in the park when you did a rainbow flick? It was amazing." She smiles to herself and I think that it may have worked. That she might sit down and remember when she used to take me to the park and play with me. How Dad would be in goal and we would take shots at him. She could do more keepie-uppies than either of us.

Maybe she has had the same memory, as I see a funny look cross her face and her tone changes. "Your dad rang earlier. I didn't get to it in time – but give him a ring back, will you?"

Mum **never** answers the phone. Always says things like "I just missed it," or "They rang off". Once, when she thought I was out, I heard the phone ringing and decided to leave it, to see if she would get it. After about ten rings I heard her scream in a scary voice, "LEAVE ME ALONE!" and then a bad swear word. So I always try to answer it super-fast now, when I'm in. To make sure I never hear that voice again.

"Anyway, I'm shattered, hon. I'm off for a lie-down."

"Don't you want some pasta?" I call after her, but it's too late. That's probably the most I will see of her this week.

I ring Dad. He starts talking quickly. It sounds like he's doing something else at the same time as talking to me.

"I know we rearranged for this weekend, Arch, but it's Scarlett's birthday tomorrow, so rather than coming over in the morning like you usually do, can you come in the afternoon? We're taking her for a surprise birthday treat!"

I open my mouth to ask if I can come for the treat too, but then I stop myself. There's no point.

"Yeah," I say. "What time?"

"Three-ish should be OK. See you tomorrow, Arch."

I'd totally forgotten that it's Scadge's birthday. They'll make such a big deal, and she'll get SOOOO many presents. Last year they decorated the whole house and even she got bored of unwrapping things. We ended up playing with the empty boxes and she seemed to enjoy that more than anything. I hid inside the biggest box and then jumped out and shouted, "HAPPY BIRTHDAY, SCADGY SCOO!" and every single time, even though she knew perfectly well that I was in there, she squealed and then shouted, "Again!" I think she would have carried on for hours, but after about twenty minutes she laughed so hard that she weed herself and Julie got really mad with me.

"For goodness' sake, Archie. Do you have to get her so wound up?"

I've not got anything for her birthday. I try to think of things in my room that I could wrap up and pretend are new. Obviously, I can take her a load of stickers, but that doesn't feel like a good enough present. I want to give her something special.

I sit down and start making her a card. Mum has never bought birthday cards, even back when she could afford them. She says, "They are an absolute waste of time, paper and money. Who in this world would not prefer a hand-drawn picture?" I loved it when we made them together. Cutting out shapes and drawing pictures of things that we knew people would like. Mum is great at drawing. She makes things look so realistic, shading with the side of the pencil. She used to draw me, a long time ago.

I rip out a page from my English notebook – I'm not at the middle page yet so I can steal the centre pages without anyone knowing. Last year I kept stealing middle pages from my topic book until it was so thin that Mr Fell said, "Has your book been on a diet, Archie?" I just went bright red and shrugged but he ruffled my hair and said, "Don't worry, Archie, I'm only messin'. I'd love to see what you wrote on all those pages. Next time leave 'em in, eh?"

As I fold the paper firmly down the middle, I know exactly what I'm going to draw. There's only one thing that Scadge ever asks me to draw, and she asks again and again. As I make the outline and start shading in the legs, I feel happy thinking about how much Scadge will like it.

It's weird having a sister and not really getting to hang out with her that much. I sometimes imagine what it would be like if I could live at Dad and Julie's and see Scadge every single day. I picture her running up and cuddling me and making me draw her pictures after school. She thinks I'm great at drawing even though I'm not. Scadge kind of thinks I'm good at everything. I hope that when she gets older, she doesn't realize how wrong she's been.

She probably won't want to hang out with me when she's older though. If Dad and Julie had their way I wouldn't see her much at all. I wish I could do something that she'll remember for ever. Something bigger than a stupid drawing.

Then I remember what Mouse said in the bus shelter about my favourite things. Scadge is one of the things on my happy list. Just as I'm colouring in the horn an idea hits me.

Surely I can't do it. Or can I? There's one person I need to ask.

I jump straight on Jack to check in with Mouse. I've still not told her about the B-B wish, and she'll kill me if I make any more wishes without checking in with her first. I'm pretty terrified of her. If you'd seen her karate-chop Henry Bude in the neck in the infants, you would be too.

"KARGHH KARGHHH!" I hoot for the second time, jumping off Jack and looking up at the window. Mouse opens the door and comes out of the house, holding Flump and covered in sawdust.

"How about a unicorn?!" I shout, before she even has time to close the door behind her.

"What are you talking about?" she says.

"You wanted me to think about what makes me happy?" I say, trying to contain my excitement.

"Yes."

"You said the next wish should be impossible, so that even YOU know it's real?"

"Yes."

"Well, I've got it. A unicorn!"

Mouse stares at me. "There are many things that could fit with this criteria, Archie. How did you jump straight into the mythical-creature realm?"

"Scadge LOVES them. It's her birthday and I've not got her a present. Can you imagine if I can magic up a unicorn? It would make her so happy! Then you'll believe me, won't you?"

"Yes, I guess so. I mean, it's slightly bonkers, but why not? When are you going to do it?"

"I'm going round there tomorrow afternoon."

"Fine. You have to come straight here when you leave on Sunday and fill me in. You're having tea with us anyway, aren't you?"

"Deal!" I say, and just as I'm about to pedal off on Jack, I turn back and add, "Oh yeah, I forgot to mention – I made wish number four already, so this will be number five."

"What did you wish for?!" she calls after me as I start pedalling. I turn back and shout over my shoulder, "Oh, nothing major. The B-Bs are going to get what they deserve, that's all!"

I hear her gasp and yell after me, "Archie! Come back! Archie!"

I let myself freewheel down the hill as the wind hits my face. My life is feeling better now. Better than before I met Lucas, when I was sad and lonely. Who needs a stupid caravan holiday when you can magic up a unicorn! *Everything is going to be OK*, I think. No, even better than that. "EVERYTHING IS GOING TO BE GREAT!" I shout at the top of my lungs into the wind.

CHAPTER TEN

Stop hoping for the rain to finish, just start dancing. —Lucas Bailey

Dancing in the playground, when it's hammering it down, in front of some wet dinner ladies and the B-B Gang, is an absolutely terrible idea, Lucas. —Archie Crumb

That night I dream about Lucas Bailey riding a unicorn. It makes me laugh out loud when I wake up, and straight away I close my eyes, swap Lucas for Scadge and picture her grinning from ear to ear on the back of a white unicorn with a rainbow-coloured horn. I keep it firmly in my mind and say, "I wish that Scadge could have her very own unicorn for her birthday."

When I open my eyes, my alarm starts beeping and I lean over to turn it off, mumbling to myself, "I didn't even set my alarm. It's Saturday!"

Then I take my wish list and update it.

ARCHIE CRUMB'S WISH LIST

1. XBOX & PIZZA
2. THE BIGGEST STICKER COLLECTION IN THE WORLD
3. ICE CREAM VAN
4. REVENGE ON THE B-B GANG
5. UNICORN FOR SCADGE
6.
7.
8.
9.

I jump out of bed, and I'm feeling so excited and happy that I decide to make pancakes to celebrate. They're Mum's favourite. When I was little, we always said that one day we would open a pancake parlour, selling pancakes with hundreds of different fillings. She taught me how to make them, how to get them super thin and flip them perfectly. It's a good job she taught me really, otherwise I would only be able to cook things from a tin, and soup, beans and spaghetti hoops sometimes get a bit boring. We were going to call it "Flippin' Good Pancakes".

My pancake-eating record is six, but I can only eat that many if they are all lemon and sugar. If I add any chocolate or banana then they're more filling. Mum always used to make me have a savoury one with cheese in, to start with, but now I make them on my own I can put whatever I like in them. That's one good thing about her being in bed – I can kind of do my own thing, make my own decisions. Sometimes when I see kids who have "normal" parents I feel sorry for them.

Once I saw this kid in the park, he must have been the same age as me. He had his skateboard under his arm and his mum was making him put on elbow and knee pads. She was so busy, fiddling and faffing and tightening his helmet for ages, behaving like he was about to go up into space. It made me think that the poor kid was definitely going to fall off the skateboard. I guess it's a bit like sending something out into the universe, but this time the mum was sending pure worry out there. It would end up making the very thing that she did not want to happen – happen. She kept trying to tell him what to do.

"Put your foot further back. Stretch your arms out for balance. Bend your knees."

I wanted to shout, "Leave him alone, lady! Let him fall off!"

Obviously, I didn't. Every time he wobbled, she would gasp or shriek. Then she wouldn't let him go down the hill. What's the point in taking him to the park with his skateboard if you're not going to let him go down a hill?!

My mum wouldn't care what hill I went down. Although Mum wouldn't come to the park with me in the first place.

As I'm mixing up the batter I keep wondering if the unicorn has arrived yet. I imagine Scadge's face when she sees it.

When I take three pancakes up to Mum, she's propped up in bed with her eyes closed.

"Pancakes!" I whisper, and put them down by the bed. She looks at me as if I'm not there at all.

Then she seems to see me properly and says, "You going to your dad's?"

"Yeah, they're away next weekend, so I'm going today instead. This afternoon."

"Why not this morning?" she asks. I can tell by the tone of her voice that she's in one of her dark moods. Sometimes when it's Dad's weekend she gets like this.

"Did he not *want* you this morning?" she spits.

"It's Scadge's birthday," I mumble.

"Is it now? I bet you can't wait. You'll go and have a *perfect* time in their *perfect* house with their *perfect* little family. Not like here, stuck with me in this state."

"Mum, you know I prefer being here with you, but I have to go."

"HAVE to! Ha!"

I take a big breath in and walk out of the room. When she's like this there's no point in trying to talk to her; she just gets really angry.

Once she started going on and on at me, saying that I hated her and avoided her. That made me feel bad. I remembered all the times that I had crept out of her room or not wanted to listen to her crying. When I told her that I was sorry she pulled the covers over her head and called me a selfish little rat. I will never forget that – the way she spat those words at me. *Selfish little rat.* It sounded like she hated me. So now, even though it feels bad walking away, I know that it'll feel worse if I stay.

I desperately want it to be half past two so that I can set off and see Scadge. I pack my bag, put in my cleanest pyjamas and the card for Scadge, and then gather up some stickers for her. I think she will love the ones that smell of sugary fruits so I put a handful of them in the front pocket along with every single unicorn sticker that I can find. Mum still hasn't noticed that my room is now basically one huge pile of stickers with a tiny path to the bed.

At two I sling my bag over my shoulder, shout, "Bye!" to Mum, who doesn't answer, and then jump on Jack and start the ride over to Dad's. I'll be a bit early but they'll just have to put up with that.

About halfway there, as I'm cutting through the estate, a gust of wind nearly blows me off my seat and a bright red leaf hits me in the face. My bike starts wobbling and I'm worried that I'm going to land on my face again, but I manage to control the weaving handlebars and the leaf blows from my face and up into the air. There's a tingling in my spine and I know at that moment that my wish has come true.

I pedal even faster and can feel my heart beating in my chest, my cheeks stinging with the cold air. I can't wait to see Scadge's face. I have no idea what's going to be there when I arrive but whatever it is, it's going to be amazing! There could be crowds of people, television crews desperate to catch a glimpse. We could become famous. The first people to ever find a real-life unicorn!

As I pull up at Dad's, I feel giddy with excitement. Everything looks normal, no crowds or cameras. I wonder if maybe this will be the one that doesn't work, but then I look through the front window and see Dad and Julie shouting at each other, their arms moving angrily. I hear Dad shout, "Of course I didn't buy the stupid thing! I don't know where it came from!"

I smile to myself. It's happened!

When I knock on the door, I hear Julie hiss, "Oh, perfect, and now Archie's here! Just what we need." Dad shushes her and opens the door with a big fake smile on his face.

"Archie! Lovely to see you, buddy."

Liar, I think.

"You're early!" says Julie, with an even worse fake smile on her lips.

"Where's Scadge?" I ask, wanting to get away from them both as quick as I can.

"SCARLETT's in the back garden," Julie says.

"We've had a bit of a day, to be honest, Archie.

She's quite overexcited so don't wind her up, will you?" As I walk towards the back door Dad adds, "When we got back from the adventure playground there was a bit of a shock waiting in the garden. Me and Julie need to figure out what to do with it and in the meantime if you can watch them both, that would be great, son."

"Sure!" I say, trying to disguise my excitement.

I open the door, expecting my mind to be blown by something magical, something impossible, something that has never been seen before. I almost expect music to start playing and glitter to start falling from the sky. When I look into the garden, first I see Scadge singing a song with an expression of total rapture on her face, then I follow her eyes to what looks like a small Shetland pony with what is quite clearly a cardboard horn strapped to its head. I look more closely at the horn and see that it's attached by a piece of elastic and is coming off the pony's head at a jaunty angle. I don't know whether to laugh or feel cheated. Scadge looks up at me, pure joy shining in her eyes.

"Archie, it happened!" she squeals. "My birthday wish came true! Isn't she the most beautiful thing you've ever seen?!"

And I realize that a wish coming true can mean totally different things for different people. This may not be my idea of a unicorn, but to Scadge there is nothing more real than the unicorn standing in front of her. It's magic.

"Yes, she is," I say. "What's her name?"

"Mystical Magical Sparkles the Third."

"Good name."

"Can you believe it?" she asks.

"No, I can't quite believe it," I say as Mystical Magical Sparkles the Third does what looks like her fourth enormous pile of poo on the tiny and perfectly manicured lawn.

"I told you that unicorns were real," says Scadge seriously.

"I did not know that unicorns pooed so much, did you?"

"No!" she says excitedly, as if unicorn poo was the best thing in the world. "And she does massive big unicorn wee-wees that make Mummy VERY angry. I LOVE her."

"Do you want to sit on her back?"

"Yes!"

As I'm lifting her up high, I hear a loud banging on the window and see Julie's angry face. She's waving her hands about and shouting something. I give her a cheerful wave and lift Scadge up on top of her very own cardboard-horned unicorn.

"Enjoy every second!" I whisper into her little ear. "Take a picture in your mind and remember it for ever." I see her blinking her eyes shut like the shutter on a camera, trying to store the picture in her mind, and I know that she'll never forget this birthday.

"Whenever something feels impossible, you can remember this, can't you? That picture in your head can remind you that ANYTHING is possible."

It makes me feel so good to know that it was me who did this for her.

"Hold on tight!" I say, and Mystical Magical Sparkles the Third bends her head low to munch on the perfect lawn.

Then Julie storms into the garden in her pristine white dress.

"Get off that creature immediately. We don't know where it came from. It could be riddled with disease!" I'm not sure that Shetland ponies are known for having many diseases and I'm about to say as much, but Julie looks so furious I decide to keep quiet. As she heads towards us, she doesn't see the latest steaming pile from Mystical Magical Sparkles the

Third and ends up skidding through it and landing on her bum.

"This is definitely the best wish ever..." I whisper to Scadge with a giggle, and she wraps her little arms around my neck in agreement.

CHAPTER ELEVEN

It doesn't matter what happens to you, it's all about your reaction. —Lucas Bailey

Once, an old lady gave me an olive and I spat it back out into her hand. —Archie Crumb

"So it wasn't *actually* a unicorn?" says Mouse, when I tell her on Sunday teatime. We're sitting on her bed, about to watch yesterday's match, Flump nestled between us.

"Well, no, not *technically*, but in Scadge's head it was totally real and so my wish did come true. You should have seen Dad's and Julie's faces. It was hilarious."

"What are they going to do with it?"

"Julie rang every single farm for miles and no one was missing a pony! It was brilliant, she kept saying, 'Well, it's not been magicked up from thin air.' I felt like telling her that actually there's quite a big chance that is has! Eventually she found an animal shelter and they're picking it up tomorrow. The lady was really nice and says that Scadge can visit it whenever she wants."

"I'm still not convinced that this proves anything."

"How else would it have got there?" I say, a little bit too loudly for Flump, who buries herself under my knee.

"I don't know! Maybe it was a joke from one of Julie's family? Maybe it wandered out of someone else's garden and ended up at your dad's?"

"Oh, and it just happened to have a horn strapped to its head?"

"I'm sure there are poor ponies all over the land who are being dressed up like unicorns as we speak. That's certainly not proof your wishes are coming true."

"Well, I believe it!" I say, and then immediately start wondering if I actually do. Mouse has a way of making me question everything. I can see why she wants to be a lawyer when she grows up. She could argue about ANYTHING. If she wanted to make me believe that my name wasn't Archie Crumb, I'm pretty sure she could do it.

"That means you only have four wishes left. I think that you need to be careful how you word your next ones. You could end up expecting one thing and getting something totally different. A unicorn and a pony with a cardboard horn are two very different things."

"Not to Scadge," I say.

"Yes, but you know what they say – be careful what you wish for!"

"Well, I did pretty good with the B-B wish. You wait till Monday. I don't think they are going to be mean to us for much longer."

"Oh yes! What did you wish for **exactly**?"

"I wished for revenge!" I say, adding a big fake evil laugh.

"But what were your words, Archie?"

"That people would laugh at them for a change, or that they knew what it was like to be laughed at, or... Oh, I can't remember. But it will be good, I promise."

As I'm pedalling home on Jack, with a warm Tupperware of lasagne in my rucksack, I start thinking about my next wish. I think I should wait until I'm **really** sure about what I want this time. Mouse is right, the wording is super important. How would I have made sure I got a real unicorn? Maybe if I had said, "I wish Scadge got a **real** unicorn for her birthday like in the storybooks," rather than, "I wish Scadge got a unicorn," it would have worked. It's so complicated, this wishing business. You have to know exactly what you want in the first place.

When I get in, the house seems dimmed and sad, the way it always does after an evening at Mouse's. The musty smell in the living room is getting worse and I can see a damp mouldy patch growing on the wall. I half wonder whether I should wish for a new house, but I actually quite like this one. It would just be nice if it felt like how it used to, before Mum and Dad started arguing, before Julie.

It used to feel warm and safe, Mum pottering about, knowing that someone was always downstairs when I went to bed, lolling on Dad's knee watching football on telly. I didn't understand the game properly; I wouldn't have known what offside even was. I just wanted to be with Dad. There weren't black dots of mould on the walls then. It's as though the house knows that we're not happy.

Still, if I wish that Mum and Dad had never split

up, that would be the end of Scadge so I can't do that. There are some things that wishes can't fix. Then I look at the mould and think, *There are some things that I can fix. Things that I don't need to wish for. I can make them happen without magic.* I spend the rest of the evening wobbling on the back of the sofa scrubbing at the mouldy patch with a soapy sponge until I can't see it any more. I smile to myself. It feels good.

On Monday morning, as I'm saying bye to Mouse and walking into class, Bella and Bea trip me up. I fall over their feet and bang my nose hard on Felix Ratton's table. Blood starts pouring from my nostrils and the whole class gather around to see the drama. Kids from the corridor all stand in the doorway looking in at the mess.

"Poor Archie Crumb," taunts Bea as she and Bella link arms and lean over me, grinning smugly.

As I stand up and try to stop any more blood from hitting the floor, I feel it. A little shiver goes down my spine and one of the windows rattles in the wind.

"Why don't you help him up, Bea? If you feel so sorry for him." Then Bella playfully shoves Bea towards me with their arms still linked together.

Bea takes a step forward and doesn't see the pool of blood under her foot. She slips and falls to the floor, taking Bella with her. I hear a gasp from the crowd as they hit the floor and then it happens. The room is silent, and as they both get to their knees to stand back up, it rings out for the whole crowd to hear loud and clear:

PRRRRFFFFFFFFFFFFFFFFFFFT.

The loudest fart I have ever heard.

After a moment of shocked silence there are shrieks, howls and whoops. No one knows which of the B-Bs did it and no one seems to care. Raspberries are being blown, there is pointing and laughing. I see Mouse at the door; she winks at me and mouths, "Are you OK?" I nod and wink back. I can hear people making new names for the B-Bs.

"The Butt Blowers!"

"The Bottom Burpers!"

"The Blow-Off Babes!"

Both Bella and Bea have turned bright red in the face. For a moment they look lost, as though they have no idea how to handle this, and then Bella's eyes go steely and she makes a choice.

"Erggh, Bea, that stinks!" she says loud enough for most of the room to hear. People sniff the air and the groans start coming. Everyone's holding their noses or putting their heads into their T-shirts. Bella quickly stands and as she takes a huge step away from Bea another huge fart fills the air:

PRRRRFFFFFFFFFFFFFFFFFFFFT.

This time clearly coming from Bella. The crowd turn on her, laughing hysterically and pointing.

"MOVE ALONG! GET TO YOUR CLASSROOMS, PLEASE." Mrs Mather's voice cuts through the gathering at the door.

"Oh my goodness!" she says as she sees the blood on the floor. "What happened here?"

"He tripped over my foot, miss, honest!" says Bella immediately. "And then Bea slipped in the blood and farted." Everyone giggles and Bella looks victorious.

I think, *I can't change people on the inside.*

Then Mouse squeezes into the classroom and brings me some toilet roll for my nose.

"Amazing!" she whispers, as we both look over and giggle at the bright red, scowling faces of the not so powerful B-B Gang.

CHAPTER TWELVE

To me a champion is someone who – even
when no one is watching – has their head
down and just keeps going through the
sweat and pain. –Lucas Bailey

If I'm in sweaty pain, I put my head down
and ask for a bath and some paracetamol!
–Archie Crumb

On the day of the football trials, when I do the
squawk, Mouse comes out with her lucky kit on.

"I've got a good feeling about today, Archie! I think
this could be my time to shine!"

"I thought you said they won't pick you because
you're the only girl."

"Yeah, but since then I've written a speech on

gender equality in sport, which I'm going to give in assembly! Let's see if they can ignore me after this!"

"No one can ignore you, Mouse, that's for sure," I say as we head up the road. I start thinking about the trials and a feeling of dread comes over me.

Last night I took a football to the waste patch at the end of our road to practise. Instead of sitting in my room panicking about the trials I thought I should go and do something – see how good or bad at football I really am.

When I got there, I tried to do some kick ups and at first I was OK without the sneering faces of the others waiting for me to make a mistake. I'm always better when I'm on my own or with Mouse. I even beat my personal best of four. But a little voice in my head kept creeping in.

You are not good enough.

You'll never make the tournament.

They don't even let you play at lunchtime.

With each bad thought I missed the ball or kicked it way too hard, and that just made the voices get even louder. I feel like I'm now even *worse* at football, if that's possible.

When we get to the bus shelter, Mouse makes me sit down and watch a full rehearsal of her speech. As she's listing famous sportswomen, her voice rising to a passionate shout, a little old lady with a shopping trolley on wheels comes and sits in the shelter next to me. You would think that would make Mouse stop, or at least lower her voice, but no, it only encourages Mouse more and the lady gets the full focus of Mouse's energy.

"These women, who have sacrificed so much to get to the top, deserve more from the younger generation."

The little old lady looks at me and smiles. She seems happy enough to have joined the show. Then Mouse lowers her voice and goes off script, in an attempt to win the old lady's vote.

"You didn't live your life only to find that nothing has been learned, that women may have got the vote and found a way into the workplace, only to be told, 'That's it, enough's enough, ladies, there are still things that you just can't do – men are bigger than you. They are stronger than you. It's a physical fact. Know your place.'"

The old lady gets a packet of dates out of the shopping trolley and offers me one, I remember the olive incident and decline. Mouse continues, "I, for one, am sick of it! Girls need to be celebrated, championed and encouraged to get involved. There's no such thing as girls' sport or boys' sport. We need to get rid of this outdated attitude, which still creeps into our education today. LET US PLAY!!"

Me and the old lady start clapping.

"Well done, dear," says the lady. "Is that for the school play? It was lovely."

In assembly Mouse gives it everything she's got. The speech is amazing and the whole school start stamping their feet at the end and the girls start whooping really loudly. She takes an over-the-top bow, but when she comes off the stage, I can see that she's not happy.

"Where's Mr Fell?" she whispers as she squeezes in next to me. "He saw my speech, didn't he?" I look around and realize that the only teacher in the hall is Miss Crowther, a tiny lady who speaks in a whisper and teaches the reception class. She's too busy looking at her iPad to have heard any of the speech. I can see how upset Mouse is. I really want to do something.

I lean over and whisper, "I could just..." Mouse knows exactly what I'm thinking.

"No! Archie, that's cheating. I want to get into that tournament because I'm good at football. Promise me you won't make a wish – for either of us. Promise?"

"OK, I promise," I say sadly.

*

After school, at the trial, we're put into groups of five and Mr Fell says, "You'll all have at least three mini-matches to show me what you've got. At the end of the session, I'll have a list of seven players and two subs."

Loads of kids have come to watch. Bella is sitting at one end of the playground and Bea is at the other. They've not spoken since the farts.

I look around at Jayden Thomas, Kit Parsons and Sol Redfern all warming up. Jiggling up and down on their tiptoes, looking like proper footballers. I try and jiggle too but my jiggling doesn't really have any rhythm and I look like I'm having some kind of fit so I stop. I see Mouse in her kit looking serious. She stretches her legs in front of her, as professional as any of the boys. Just as I'm thinking that there's really no point in being here, Mr Fell pats me on the head and says, "Archie, you're a five. OK, all the ones over there, twos there, threes there, fours by the net and fives stay here. These are your teams. You've got five minutes to warm up and decide where you're playing." As soon as he says this, I know immediately that I'll end up in goal. No one EVER wants to be in goal. There's no joy being a keeper – if you win, no one thinks it was down to you and if you lose everyone blames you. Just as I'm thinking this, Kit

Parsons looks at me and says, "You're in net, all right?"

Mouse is huddling with her team and Jayden Thomas is doing most of the talking. Jayden is pretty mean. He is an honorary member of the B-B Gang since he started going out with Bella. I don't know what "going out" even means. I don't think that they actually ever "go" anywhere. All I ever see them doing is shoving each other around the playground and then laughing at other kids. Yesterday in the dinner hall Bella shoved him right into me and Mouse, and then said, "You touched them! That means I can't go near you for a week!" Then she ran off giggling. I can see that Mouse isn't happy to be on his team. Mr Fell blows the whistle and the games begin.

Two matches down and my team have won one and lost one. I've let in a few goals, but so far I've not completely embarrassed myself. I'm focusing on shouting encouragement to the rest of the team like I've seen keepers do on telly. I'm remembering all of the quotes from my stickers.

"Believe in yourself, Kit! You can do it!"

"Keep trying! Don't give up!"

"Teamwork makes the dream work!"

I'm not sure if it works but we don't do badly and

no one tells me to shut up. If anything, it makes me feel a bit useful, and I don't feel so bad about the goals that I let in. At the end of each game, we all get into a huddle and pat each other on the backs, though no one really says anything. I think of all the post-match interviews I've seen with the Valley Rovers manager and try and copy him.

"We're doing great. I really think you can all get on to this team if you keep trying as hard as you have been. Only one more game to go and Mr Fell is watching. Make it count." It seems to work, and they all start patting each other even harder on the back and shouting things like, "Yes!"

"Come on!"

"We can do this!"

Our last game is against Mouse's team. She's looking a bit fed up and when she walks on to the pitch she mumbles, "Jayden Thomas told the others not to pass it to me."

The whistle blows and Kit immediately takes the ball and scores. By the final minute of the game we are winning 5–4 and Mouse is really upset. No one on her team seems to notice that she's there. She's shouting for them to pass but they just completely ignore her. I don't see her touch the ball once. Mr Fell looks at his watch and is about to blow the whistle. I really want Mouse to be on the team; she looks so sad and it all feels so unfair. As their keeper takes the last goal kick of the game it all happens at once. He miskicks the ball and it rolls towards Mouse. *This is my moment*, I think. I know I made a promise but this feels too important. I *have* to wish for her to make the team, she deserves it so much. I try to imagine Mouse at the tournament but all I can picture is myself standing triumphantly next to Lucas Bailey. I shake my head and try to get the right picture in my mind but my stupid face keeps popping up, soaking up the roar of the crowd, grinning with a trophy in my hands. Just as she's about to kick the ball, I try and say it out loud, but the wrong words come out and instead of saying, "I wish *Mouse* could play in the tournament," I say, "I wish *I* could play in the tournament." At that moment, as her foot touches the ball, a huge gust of wind blows and knocks her off balance. She hoofs the ball up into the air, lands hard on her bum and I can see all the others giggling. Jayden Thomas makes contact with the ball and then, after a couple of nifty touches, boots it my way. The ball seems to slow down in mid-air. It's heading for the top right corner and I know that I can get to it in time. I'm at full stretch and

I feel like a pro. The tips of my gloves just touch the ball and nudge it over the crossbar. It's the best save I have ever made in my life. The whistle blows and my team come and congratulate me. Beyond them I can see Mouse scowling at me and shaking her head. She knows. She knows that only magic could make me save a goal like that.

In all of the years that she's been taking penalties at me in her back garden, I have never once moved the way I just did. Forget unicorns and ice cream vans, me being good at football for one split second is enough to convince Mouse that this is no coincidence, that magic is in the air. I think back to the promise I made her this morning. What have I done?

When Mr Fell is reading out the chosen players, I can feel her eyes on me the whole time. All of the obvious ones make it; Kit, Jayden and Dan Dore are all on the list. Then he gets to the subs.

"The first sub is Brendan for some brilliant defending." I breathe a sigh of relief; maybe this wish didn't work. Maybe he won't say my name. "And the second sub, not only because of his miraculous last-minute save, but because of his team spirit and positive attitude, is. . ." *Don't say it, please don't say it.* I look at Mouse and then put my head into my hands as he says, "Archie Crumb." When I lift my head to look back at Mouse, I see the back of her lucky shirt walking away.

She'll never forgive me.

CHAPTER THIRTEEN

You have the power to be incredible, just
the way you are. —Lucas Bailey

My trousers are too small and I'm wearing
a T-shirt with spaghetti hoop juice on it —
that's "just the way I am". —Archie Crumb

"It was an accident!" I call. I'm trying to keep up with
Mouse as she steams ahead of me down the cobbles.
She hasn't looked back once and I can barely keep up
with her.

"I didn't mean to do it, honest," I shout. "I was
trying to wish for *you* to make the team, but it came out
wrong." She stops suddenly, turns and walks back up
the hill towards me. The furious look on her face makes
me wish that I was still looking at the back of her head.

"So, instead of saying, 'I wish *Mouse* could get on the team like she TOTALLY DESERVES', you said, 'I wish *I* could get on the team even though I'm terrible at football.'"

"Yes!" I say, relieved that she finally seems to be understanding. It doesn't seem to make her feel any better though and she carries on.

"You heard my speech. You knew how important this was to me. You promised!"

"I know, I'm sorry," I mumble.

"I guess it just shows what kind of friend you really are, Archie. Maybe that's not the kind of friend I want in my life. Thanks for nothing."

"It was an accident!"

"No, Archie, it was **you**! You said it. You imagined it. You actually have control over your own life."

"But I. . ."

"I know things aren't easy for you, Archie. But you could have wished for *anything*. And you wished for something selfish."

"You have no idea how hard it is being awful at absolutely everything!" I say.

"Maybe you're so bad at everything because you keep telling yourself you are. Stop feeling sorry for yourself – it's boring." She spits these last words and they sound horrible, like something Bella would say to me, or Mum when she's having a bad day. I never thought that Mouse would make me feel like that.

Anger starts building inside me and I'm not just talking to her, I'm talking to Bella and Bea and Mum and Dad and everyone who has ever made me feel bad.

"Easy for you to say – in your perfect house with your perfect parents. Maybe you're not such a good friend either, Mouse. Do you ever wonder what it's actually like for me when I go home? No – because you don't really care. You just pretend that you don't notice that I don't have enough money for clothes that fit. You NEVER ask about my completely broken mother any more. You don't listen when my tummy's rumbling because I'm starving. Maybe I don't need *you* as a friend either!"

We are both silent. "I don't ask, Archie, because I don't want to make you feel bad," she says at last, in a very quiet voice. "But if that's how you see it then I guess we really can't be friends any more." She turns and walks into her house without looking back and closes the door behind her.

All the anger has gone and I feel sick. Me and Mouse never fall out, apart from the time we were six and I accidentally sat on Flump. She was fine but Mouse got really cross and didn't speak to me for a whole day.

Afterwards, when she said sorry, her mum told me that Mouse's granddad was poorly and she wasn't really cross about me sitting on Flump, she was just upset about that and took it out on me. It's weird how sometimes people are sad about one thing but then get cross about all sorts of other things. Like when Mum called me a *selfish rat*. I think she was sad about something else, but I can't be sure.

Mouse certainly seems angry with me, that much I know.

I kick my feet along the floor and head towards home but when I get to the front door, I really don't want to go in. Sometimes I feel lonelier inside my house than I do outside, so I keep walking.

I head towards the bus shelter and sit down. I feel lonely everywhere, I think. Even round at Mouse's. I sit at their dinner table eating her mum's curry and listen to them teasing each other and I feel on the outside. In class, too, when I'm surrounded by thirty other kids all putting their hands up and chattering to each other. They all seem so different to me.

Being at home, knowing my mum's up in bed,

makes me feel super lonely, and my dad's fake smiles and lies make me feel isolated at his house too.

Through the grubby glass of the shelter, I see a group of teenagers all laughing and chucking a traffic cone in the air. I wonder if anyone in the world feels like me. Heat rises in my cheeks and there's a dull ache in my throat. I don't want to be like Mum, always crying at everything, and so I force the ache down and take a big breath in.

"Archie! I thought it was you."

I look up. It's Julie, wearing her pink running gear. She keeps jogging on the spot as she looks at me. The lump in my throat hasn't quite gone away and I don't trust myself to speak so I just half-smile instead.

"Are you waiting for the bus?" she asks as she jogs.

"No," I mumble.

I can tell that she doesn't know what to say now. I wonder if she'll make the sigh/laugh noise and think that it will sound even weirder when she's jogging.

"OK, well, see you soon, Archie." She waves and jogs on.

"Have a nice time at the caravan," I mumble, and instantly regret it as the lump pops straight back up into my throat.

She slows down and turns back to me.

"Does your mum know you're out on your own?" she says.

"I'm not a baby," I say under my breath.

"I know. I'm sorry. You just look so. . ."

"I'm fine. Enjoy your run."

"Well, if you're sure you're OK?"

I nod and then stop looking at her until I hear her sigh and jog away. I'm left alone again, with no friends, no family who care about me and a massive lump in my throat.

CHAPTER FOURTEEN

Aim high. You might even hit the moon.
—Lucas Bailey

The last time I took a penalty, I tripped
over the ball and it didn't even make
it to the net, let alone to the moon!
—Archie Crumb

With Mouse ignoring me, school is even worse than usual, and then the weekend seems to drag on for ever.

After updating my wish list:

ARCHIE CRUMB'S WISH LIST

1. XBOX & PIZZA

2. THE BIGGEST STICKER COLLECTION IN THE WORLD
3. ICE CREAM VAN
4. REVENGE ON THE B-B GANG
5. UNICORN FOR SCADGE
6. GET PICKED FOR THE FOOTBALL TOURNAMENT
7.
8.
9.

I decide I need to tackle the sticker mountain and spend the whole weekend sorting my stickers into categories.

ANIMALS
FOOTBALL
DISNEY
SMELLY
PUFFY
MARVEL

I don't know how I'll sell them without Mouse. Maybe she was right; the reason that I'm rubbish at everything might be because I tell myself I am. Maybe I need to start telling myself a different story.

"I could sell loads of stickers on my own," I say out loud, not quite believing it. Then I try out some more positive things:

"I AM good at football."

"I AM good at drawing."

"I AM good at maths." I pause and think about Mouse.

"I AM a good friend," I say to myself. I get a Lucas sticker and tell him: "I am a good friend, Lucas. Maybe I haven't been, but I **want** to be and that's the main thing, isn't it?"

He just looks at me, with his kind, amused expression. I know what he'd tell me if he was in front of me now. That I need to *do* something, not just sit around wishing and waiting.

I jump up and head out on Jack. I need to see Mouse and make this right – and it might take more than a wish.

"KARGHH KARGHHH," I squawk, for the fifth time. Just as I'm about to give up and turn Jack around, the front door opens, but it's not Mouse. It's Zoe.

"She won't come out, Archie, I'm afraid. No matter how much you squawk."

"OK. Sorry," I say. "I'll go home then."

She comes out of the front door. "What's happened with you two?"

"I did something stupid," I mumble.

She nods, but she looks kind. "I'd love for you two to make it up. I know she seems like a tough cookie, Arch, but she's a softie deep down. She needs you as much as you need her, you know."

"I know," I say, swallowing hard. What if me, my stupid wishes and my big mouth have ruined the one friendship I've ever had? What if Mouse never speaks to me again and I end up alone and sad and spend all day in bed crying?

"Why don't you try tomorrow," Zoe says gently, "when she's calmed down a bit? You can tell her you're sorry."

I nod, unable to speak, and turn Jack around.

"Wait a sec, Arch," Zoe says. "There's something else I want to talk to you about."

But I don't stop. I pretend I don't hear her and cycle off, wind in my face.

Back at home, sitting on the sofa with a tin of spaghetti hoops, I'm feeling sorry for myself. I imagine Dad, Julie and Scadge all in the caravan having a lovely weekend and I feel worse. I imagine my life without Mouse in it and I feel more sorry for myself. I imagine being stuck in this dirty house with my mum up in bed for the rest of my life and I feel EVEN MORE sorry for myself.

I think about what I said to Mouse and what she said to me. For the first time, I wonder whether we should stop being friends. Maybe I meant everything I said. Mouse can't ever know what it's like for me. How could she? Her life is so different to mine. I need someone a bit more like me. Maybe that's it!

I don't have to feel lonely, do I? I don't need Mouse or Dad or Julie or Scadge or Mum. My wishes can't change anyone on the inside, but maybe I could magic up someone brand new, who understands me. A real best friend. Someone just like me, who gets it.

Now, Archie, I think, *make sure you get the words just right.* I sit in silence for a few minutes planning what I am going to say, and then I close my eyes.

"I WISH I COULD MEET SOMEONE JUST LIKE ME, ANOTHER ARCHIE CRUMB."

I thought wishing would make me feel better, but as I open my eyes none of the bad feelings have gone away. I take Lucas out of my pocket.

"Lucas, I know I can't wish for it, but is there any way I can change myself on the inside?" I look at him for a minute and think about it. "There *has* to be," I say. "Otherwise everyone who ever felt sad would feel sad for ever." Then I rummage around in my pocket and take out the empty sticker wrapper. I smooth it out and there it is, Lucas's answer to my question. His inspiring words printed just for this moment.

YOU CAN'T ALWAYS AIM FOR HAPPINESS BUT YOU CAN AIM FOR HOPE.

I put the spaghetti down and try my hardest to get rid of my sadness and transform it into something else. I definitely can't imagine feeling "happy", so, just like Lucas says, I try to turn it into hope. If I can do this, I really am magic.

I take the sad thoughts – the caravan, Mum in bed, Mouse's hurt and angry face – and replace them with something else. Things that give me hope. I think about Mouse lying on the floor of the ice cream van, giggling and covered in chocolate sauce. I think of Scadge's look of wonder as she stroked her unicorn. I think of Lucas Bailey and the crowd going wild every time he scores a winning goal.

It starts to work. I make the pictures that make me sad fade away and the ones that make me hopeful become more vivid. Like I'm painting a picture in my head of all the things I want to see and am rubbing out all of the things that I don't. When the sad feeling in my tummy has gone and I almost feel happy it seems like magic, like maybe now I'm making my own wishes come true.

CHAPTER FIFTEEN

If you see someone with a frown, give them a smile. —Lucas Bailey

I tried this with Bella when she was scowling at me and she called me a grinning idiot. —Archie Crumb

The whole way to school the next morning I'm waiting for a gust of wind, a tingle down my spine and a boy to step out and walk by my side. Someone who gets what I'm thinking without me even having to say anything. Someone who laughs at the same jokes and collects stickers.

I pass Mouse's and do the squawk, just in case she's forgiven me, hoping that she'll appear and everything will be normal again. The door stays shut and as I squawk for the second time the window next door opens and the grumpy man sticks his head out.

"I thought I told you before to stop making that ruddy noise? She's already gone anyway so you can ruddy go away."

I drag my feet the rest of the way to school. I look out for Mouse in the bus shelter and then in the playground but can't see her anywhere.

We have another maths test in the morning and I don't know the answer to a single question. I can feel my face going red as we pass our answer sheets to the front. I think about Mouse's theory. If the reason that I'm bad at everything is because I tell myself I am, then what about this? I could tell myself all day long that I was a maths genius and still get zero out of twenty. I'm pretty sure there's no amount of positive thinking that could change that, and I'm definitely not about to waste a wish on boring old maths!

After morning break Mrs Mather comes in and claps her hands. That's when I feel it – a flicker of excitement down my spine. I look out of the window and see the leaves swirling around the playground and I know that something's about to happen.

"Thank you, thank you, everyone. Settle down." Everyone eventually stops shuffling and she carries on. "We have a new student joining us today." Then she looks right at me. "It's actually a remarkable coincidence – our new student has the SAME NAME as one of you!"

I feel as if my face is on fire. That's not really what I meant! I remember my wish: *I wish I could meet someone just like me, another Archie Crumb.*

Mrs Mather continues, "They also have the same birthday! On paper they are JUST LIKE ONE OF YOU!"

I edge forward on my seat, wondering if my long-lost identical twin is about to walk out in front of me, another skinny boy with a wonky haircut, wearing trousers that don't fit. "I want you all to make him feel very welcome. Everyone, meet Archie Crumb!"

As she says this, everyone starts giggling and whispering and looking at me. Then Mrs Jain walks in with a really tall boy who looks much older than any of us. He has muscles on his arms and it even looks like he has a moustache. On paper he is "just like me" but off paper he is nothing like me. I stare at him. He gives us all a half-wave.

Then Mrs Mather says, "Now, Archie, seeing as you have another Archie Crumb in the class, maybe you should go and sit next to him. I'm sure you'll want to get to know each other."

She points me out, and Archie Crumb walks over.

"Hi," I squeak to Archie Crumb.

"Hi," Archie Crumb says back to me in a low, confident voice, sitting down next to me.

The other Archie Crumb doesn't seem to be too shocked that there is a smaller, paler and skinnier version of himself sitting in the classroom. I guess they must have already told him about my existence.

"So your birthday is on the 27th of January as well?" I say, trying to bring my voice down to a normal pitch, but going far too low and somehow sounding like I'm doing an impression of an old man.

"Yeah, it's pretty nuts, isn't it?" The other Archie Crumb has an accent that I've never heard before.

"Where did you used to live?" I whisper as Mrs Mather starts the register.

"Birmingham," he whispers, "but Mum lost her job and so we decided to move."

His mum lost her job too – just like mine! Before I can ask him any more, I hear Mrs Mather call out our name. We both say yes at the same time and everyone laughs. Maybe this is exactly what I needed, someone just like me – but bigger, cooler and stronger. Maybe the other Archie Crumb can protect me, like my own personal bodyguard.

When the bell goes for lunch Mrs Mather asks me to show him around.

"Give him all the inside info. From one Archie Crumb to another," she says, smiling to herself. I imagine her telling her family when she gets home that a bigger, better version of an Archie Crumb arrived at school today. Them all laughing at me, saying, "Poor little Archie Crumb."

"Let's go, Arch. I'm starving," the other Archie says. He pats me on the back and I nearly go flying. He really is massive.

As we sit eating our lunch I keep staring at his moustache. I can't help it. I wonder if it's soft or spiky. Everyone in the dinner hall is looking at us. I can see some girls on the next table whispering and pointing, but not in a bad way. They seem *fascinated* by him.

I would hate being a new kid. You get so much attention for the first week, everyone pointing and fussing and trying to be your friend, and then everyone loses interest as soon as the novelty wears off. You just become another kid. The same as everyone else. It must be like being in a famous pop group that just has one hit and then never has another good song again.

Archie's telling me about his teacher from his old school. "He was such a try-hard," he says. Then he does an impression of him sitting backwards on his chair. "So, kids, let's get rid of the formality, let's tear up the rule book – everyone call me Greg."

The way he says "Greg" is really funny and I'm laughing when Mouse walks past with her tray and sees us. Her face looks hurt and sad. I want to go after her and say that I'm sorry and I made a mistake at the football – and might have made another one with Archie! – but it's too late, she's already gone to sit at the other side of the dinner hall.

I look at Archie and his moustache, sitting there eating his sandwich. He carries on making jokes about his old school and soon the girls from the next table over are giggling along. I think that Archie might have hit after hit. The novelty might never wear off. He's so cool.

After lunch I take him to the football pitch and on the way, I tell him all of the school rules. Not the official ones – the stupid hidden rules that no one tells you – until you break them by accident:

1. Never do your top button up – people

call you names if you do. I don't know why. Most people snip off their buttons to make sure they're not even tempted.

2. Don't put your hand up for every question – even if you know the answer. Bella and Bea are almost as mean to those kids as they are to ones who don't know any of the answers – like me.

3. Don't use the top corridor toilets after lunch. (Someone always leaves poo smeared on the seat – and once, before I knew, I sat down in it. It was disgusting.

4. Don't eat the carrots at lunch – they're horrible. When Timmy Tompkins ate all his carrots everyone called him "Wet Carrot" for about a month and he's still known as Carrot now.

The other Archie Crumb laughs at all of this and says, "It was the same in my last school. Kids can be idiots, can't they?"

When we get to the pitch, Dan Dore sees us and shouts over, "You two want a game?"

Then Jayden Thomas says, "New boy, you can be on our team." He looks at me and adds, "Soz,

Crumby, no more space."

I watch the boy who is just like me, yet not at all like me, jog off and say over his shoulder, "Cheers, Arch." Then he expertly flicks the ball up in front of him and strikes it hard into the net, provoking cheers from his teammates and shouts of, "Yes, Archie, yes!" I see him laughing and high-fiving the others and looking completely relaxed, as though he's been here for ever.

He may have the same name and birthday as me, but this Archie Crumb is nothing like me really. I instantly start to miss Mouse again and look around hoping to spot her but she's nowhere to be seen.

After that, all the kids decide to call me Crumby so that they can tell the difference between us. How do some kids just seem to fit in straight away? It's not fair. My last two wishes have totally backfired. I now feel even more alone than ever.

After school as I'm walking past the car park I see Bella waiting on her own. Then a big silver Mercedes pulls in and a big man in a suit gets out. I slow down my walking and watch them carefully.

"I've had to leave a meeting for this, Bella. I don't know why you want to start this daft club anyway," her dad says as he puts her bag in the boot.

"Sorry, Dad. I thought Mum was taking me," Bella

mumbles. It's the first time I have ever heard Bella use the word *sorry*. She looks different with her dad. Smaller somehow. She's seemed smaller at school too since she no longer has Bea – even though she pretends to be fine.

"You are eleven years old, for goodness' sake, it's too late for you to be an Olympic gymnast." Then he snorts with laughter and she shrinks even more. "If you want to go again you'll have to walk." Then he snorts again and he looks just like Bella does when she laughs at me. "You're too big for gymnastics anyway and too clumsy." They get in the car and drive away. She sits in the back and stares out of the window. Bella clearly already knows exactly what it's like to be laughed at. She didn't need my wish to teach her that.

CHAPTER SIXTEEN

Your commitment determines your direction.
—Lucas Bailey

I don't have any sense of direction. Once I
got lost in ASDA and I couldn't find the exit
for two hours. —Archie Crumb

The week seems to drag on and on. I only have two spaces left on my wish list. Mum is feeling "exhausted" and spends the whole week in bed crying or pretending to sleep. Mouse is ignoring my calls and every time I go and do the squawk the only response I get is from her angry neighbour. When Mrs Stanley, her nice neighbour on the other side, eventually comes out and asks me if I'm OK, I know that I'd better stop squawking.

The other Archie Crumb is now the most popular boy in school. I want to tell them all that he's only here because of me. He should be **my** best friend – that was the plan. He is nice to me, but he's too busy to be my best mate. We've not really got that much in common, apart from on paper. He's amazing at football – I'm rubbish. He's confident – I'm not. People laugh at his jokes – people laugh at me. I keep trying to find out if deep down we are the same.

"I've got the biggest sticker collection in the world," I say one day when he sees me sorting out my stickers on the wall.

"What?" says the other Archie.

"I have. My bedroom's so full that I can't open my wardrobe. It's actually quite annoying."

"Why have you got so many?"

"It's a long story. I want to sell them – do you want to buy some?"

"Not really my thing, Archie," he says. He's the only one who never calls me Crumby. "I'll spread the word though."

He did spread the word, and because he is the coolest boy in school, my sticker business is booming. Year twos and threes come to me for Disney. Year fours get hooked on emojis. Fives and sixes are split into two groups – smelly stickers and football. I have stickers for EVERYONE so there's always a queue at my little spot on the wall. I almost want Mouse to see me and to tell me not to do it at school, that we were supposed to be doing it together at the bus stop. But she doesn't say anything.

In English, instead of writing my acrostic poem I jot down all of my wishes so far and think about what I would wish for if there were no rules.

ARCHIE CRUMB'S WISH LIST

1. XBOX & PIZZA
2. THE BIGGEST STICKER COLLECTION IN THE WORLD
3. ICE CREAM VAN
4. REVENGE ON THE B-B GANG
5. UNICORN FOR SCADGE
6. GET PICKED FOR THE FOOTBALL TOURNAMENT
7. THE OTHER ARCHIE CRUMB
8. Make Mouse be my friend again?
9.

After school, as I put my key in the front door I can hear the phone ringing inside. I dump my bag and run in to answer it.

"Archie, it's me," says Mouse. She sounds bunged up like she has a cold or has been crying. "Can you come over?"

"Yes!" I say. "I'll come right now. I'm so sorry, Mouse, I never meant to..."

"Don't worry, forget about it, it doesn't matter any more." I know then that something's really wrong.

"What do you mean?" I say anxiously.

"We're moving. Mum and Dad just told me. The house is for sale and we're leaving."

"I'm coming!" I shout, and put the phone down, grab my coat and jump on Jack.

Mouse CANNOT leave. There's no way that I am going to let this happen.

When I get there, I do the squawk at full volume and she opens the door immediately, as though she's been waiting.

"Can we go to the bus shelter?" she sniffs.

"Yeah, sure."

We don't say anything on the way there. Mouse has puffy eyes and pink blotches on her cheeks, the kind that happen when you have been crying for a really long time.

I have only cried once like that – when Dad left. My face looked almost bruised afterwards and my chest hurt for a couple of days. I've not cried since then. I'm too scared to – scared that if I start, the pain in my chest will come back and never go away. Now whenever I start feeling sad and my throat gets tight I shove down the sad feelings until they go away. I have found loads of tricks to stop myself crying; here are my best ones:

ARCHIE CRUMB'S WAYS TO STOP CRYING

1. **Pinch inside my arm.** Mum once saw me doing this when Dad rang and cancelled my weekend visit. She got really cross. She said that I needed to find other ways to deal with my emotions. She gave me a cushion to punch instead. To be honest, the pinching hurt anyway, so in a way it made me feel worse, not better.

2. **Spin around until I'm dizzy.** I can only do this if I am about to cry in a large area. I once did it in the kitchen when

I was making beans on toast. It was Christmas Day (Mum finds Christmas even harder than normal days). She was up in bed and said she couldn't come down and I wasn't going to Dad's till teatime. When I put some beans in the microwave for my lunch, I suddenly felt really sad, like I might cry, and so I spun myself around twenty times, but when I stopped, I staggered into the pan rack on the wall and a saucepan hit me on the head.

3. **Say the list of stickers that I need out loud.** This distracts me – but it only worked before I had the biggest collection in the world. Now it's completely useless. I was once super scared at the dentist and started to list the stickers but then Dr Maughton, the dentist, opened my mouth and stopped me from saying anything so I started listing inside my head but it didn't work properly in my head and a tear sneaked out of my left eye. I was so cross with him. I've never been back since. That

was three years ago. I open all the post anyway so I just rip the ones up from the dentist and hide them in the black bin. If I ever see Dr Maughton in the street I hide.

4. **Shout "bananas".** One time I was on my way to Dad's on Jack and my chain broke and I fell off. We were meant to be going to the cinema and so I pushed my bike as fast as I could, limping on my hurt leg. When I eventually got there, I had blood all over my trousers and I was fifteen minutes late. There was a note on the door saying, *Sorry, Arch, had to go without you. Back in a couple of hours.* As I looked at the note, I felt the feelings coming up and I squeezed the handlebars super tight and shouted at the top of my voice, "BANANAS". An old lady with a shopping trolley stopped and looked at me and I smiled and shrugged. It was a bit embarrassing, but it did the trick. I sat and waited for two hours without crying once.

Mouse says that crying is healthy and that if I don't let myself cry then it will fester and turn into something even worse. I don't agree – what could possibly be worse than that horrible feeling in my chest?

By the time we get to the bus stop we've still not said a word to one another. We can see some older kids hanging out inside the shelter and so we just keep walking, without saying anything. That's what's so special about Mouse: I've known her for so long that it's like we know what the other is thinking.

I've missed her so much. I'm about to tell her this, but before I can, she points to a wall on the other side of the road and says, "Come on."

We cross the road and sit on a wall opposite the betting shop, watching the men inside all looking up at the screens.

"So," I say eventually, "what's going on?"

"Just what I said. They are selling the house. Mum and Dad sat me down and told me. They didn't even ask, they just told me, like it wasn't up for debate. They've had the stupid estate agent round to take pictures."

"Where are you going?"

"Yewbridge, wherever that is. They said they want to get out of the city and 'live the country life' and apparently now is the perfect time, before I start secondary school. I think Mum's got some stupid idea of having chickens, like we haven't already got enough animals, and baking bread. As if chickens and bread would make me change my mind, I'm not four years old!" As she says this, I see the tears spring back up into her eyes and I have to stop myself from telling her to shout *bananas*.

"We'll just have to stop it happening," I say.

"How? Before you suggest it, I don't want anything to do with your wishes, Archie. They don't ever work the way you want them to. I know that the other Archie Crumb is something to do with one of your stupid wishes."

I feel my face going pink; she knows me so well. "I agree," I admit. "The wishes are too unpredictable for this." After a pause I add, "Sometimes you can make something happen though, not by wishing for it but by *doing* something about it."

"But what? They'll never change their minds."

I think for a minute and then it comes to me. "What if no one will buy the house? Remember that house with the big rusty green gates on South Road?

That was for sale for years. All we need to do is put off anyone who comes to look at it."

"Yes, but that place was weird. Everyone thought it was haunted!"

"Exactly!" I say.

"What do you mean, Archie?"

"Let's make a list of ways we could put people off buying your house!" I say, tearing the centre pages from my English book.

Half an hour later and me and Mouse are grinning from ear to ear.

ARCHIE AND MOUSE'S WAYS TO
PUT OFF HOUSE BUYERS

1. Make it seem haunted (weird ghost noises, moving curtains, etc.)
2. Make the house smell disgusting
3. Spread rumours that someone died there
4. Spiders, snakes, cockroaches, maggots
5. Make it cold
6. Damp
7. Creaking

By the time we're finished, no one is going to be buying Mouse's house, that's for sure!

"We've got the whole weekend to get everything we need," I say.

"I really don't want to leave!" Mouse says quietly.

"I know," I say, and we lean our heads together and stare into the betting shop in silence.

I'm glad I couldn't wish for Mouse to be my friend again. It makes it more real that it happened anyway, without the wishes.

Later that night, as I'm getting some potato waffles out of the toaster, I hear

"KARGHH KARGHHH" and find Mouse outside on her bike. "I had to sneak out. When I got home, Mum was in a cleaning frenzy. The estate agent rang and said that some stupid family couldn't wait until Monday so they are coming round to look at the house after school! We need to start the plan tomorrow, Archie."

"Don't worry, I'll sort it," I tell her. "We'll put them off, no problem."

"What shall I do?"

"Just go home and make sure they don't suspect anything. I will gather up the stuff we need after school and meet you at yours. OK?"

"Thanks, Archie. You really are the best friend ever, you know." Then as she's about to go, she stops and says, "I'm so sorry about everything I said."

"Me too. I'm sorry too," I tell her.

As I watch her ride off I feel so happy to have her back and it makes me even more determined to fix this. I need Mouse in my life.

CHAPTER SEVENTEEN

Life is like a rollercoaster: strap yourself in and enjoy the ride. —Lucas Bailey

Last time Mouse went on a rollercoaster the boy in front vomited and it hit her in the face. —Archie Crumb

After school I'm standing outside Mouse's next to the newly erected "For Sale" sign. It won't be there for long, I think. Because this house is NOT being sold. I've brought everything we need in my rucksack:

- A bag of fake spiders that I made last night out of some black cotton I pulled off an old sock. I wrapped up a little ball and then pulled out eight little stringy legs. They're not the best but from a distance they look quite spidery.

- Some stinky kippers that I bought after school with my earnings from selling thirty packets of stickers to Felix Ratton.
- The remote-control robot from James's box of stuff.

Mouse sneaks out from the side of the house, looking behind her as she heads my way.

"They wouldn't let me out, so I had to climb out of the living room window! They've gone mad! Dad's making coffee and fresh bread and Mum's on her knees scrubbing the skirting boards – she has NEVER scrubbed the skirting boards before! They've put all the animals in the shed. It's like the Queen's coming."

"Don't worry," I say firmly. "We're going to sort it. I'll stay here and when the people arrive I'll put them off before they even get inside."

"How?" she asks.

"Leave that to me. You need to tell your mum that you want to show the people round your room *on your own*. Say something about independence and responsibility, that should make them buy it. Then they won't catch you. When the people are in your room, make the robot move on its own by hiding the remote in your pocket. Tell them that it always happens and that you think there's a ghost."

"Good idea!" she says, taking the remote.

"Here are some spiders to leave around too. You can tell them that you have a big spider problem, you don't know why but the whole house is always full of spiders, massive ones." I hand her the cotton spiders. "And leave these kippers open in your room under the bed. They stink."

"Ewww, I have to sleep in there tonight!"

"It'll be worth it, Mouse. You can't leave."

She nods. As I hand over the bag, she says, "Wish me luck, Archie!"

"You don't need luck, Mouse. We can totally do this without any luck, wishes or magic." As she's turning back to the house, I remember something. "Mouse!"

She turns back, looking excited and terrified. "Yeah?"

"Sneak Flump inside and put her on your floor. No one will buy a house if they think it's got mice in it!" She gives me a nervous thumbs up and disappears around the corner.

*

171

Fifteen minutes later and a fancy-looking silver car pulls up. I'm sitting on the wall in front of the house, swinging my legs. A smart, shiny-looking man and woman get out, with a dressed-up little baby with a ribbon on her bald head. They all look like they've just been to the hairdresser's and the woman's eyelashes make her look like a doll. They look up at the house and, as she's shutting the car door, the shiny woman says, "It looks smaller than I thought it would from the outside."

"Wait until we get inside, honey, the road looks lovely."

"Oh, it *looks* lovely," I chirp up, still swinging my legs. I looked on the internet at lunchtime for reasons that make people not buy houses. There were loads of them. I just need to pick the best ones for this particular couple.

"Shame about all the crime," I say.

"Really?" says the woman, looking alarmed.

"Yeah, three houses have been broken into in the last month. That's why next door got those really fierce fighting dogs. One of them bit a kid the other day."

"Oh my gosh. How awful!" the woman says, covering her mouth with one hand and holding the baby in the bow a little tighter with the other. I know that my work here is done. I hop off the wall and make my way off down the street, glancing behind me to check on their horrified faces.

An hour later, me and Mouse are in our new spot opposite the betting shop and she's giving me the low-down on the viewing.

"Whatever you told them must have worked," she says. "They seemed pretty freaked out when they came in, and the woman kept asking about the neighbours. She didn't seem to believe Mum when she told her that Mr and Mrs Stanley were a lovely old couple and that we all get along like a house on fire, and that Bill on the other side can seem a bit grumpy but has a heart of gold really."

"What about the other stuff?" I ask.

"Well, the spiders didn't work, the guy just said something goofy like, 'I guess they keep away the flies!' but the remote-control robot made the baby cry, so I suppose that was a success, although I did feel terrible and gave her one of my teddies to take home to cheer her up. The kippers were amazing. I hid them under my bed and when I saw them sniffing the air, I told them that sometimes the whole house smells of fish and that we can't get rid of it no matter what we do. The best of the best, though, was Flumpy here!"

she says, taking the little gerbil from her pocket and handing her to me for a snuggle.

"She ran across the floor at the perfect moment and the woman screamed so loud! I jumped out of my skin. That was it, they were out of the door as fast as they could run after that."

"Amazing!" I say, cradling Flump in one hand and holding the other one up for a high five. Mouse ignores it and sighs a big sigh.

"Mum said there are two more viewings on Monday and three on Tuesday. We can't do this for all of them, can we?"

"Of course we can," I say. "I'm not letting them take my best friend away from me."

"Shall we meet here and make some plans tomorrow?"

"I can't. I'm at my dad's, but I'll be over on Sunday for tea and we can perfect our strategy then – deal?"

"Deal," she says.

Back at home when the phone rings again, I assume that it's Mouse.

"Hey, Archie!" Dad's voice says brightly.

"Hi, Dad," I say, knowing exactly what's coming, knowing I don't want to hear it.

"So, I'm just ringing about tomorrow, Archie…"
Before he has a chance to tell me some lie or excuse about why I can't come this weekend, I take the sticker packet out of my pocket and make a crackling noise with it next to the phone.

"Oh, no, Dad, I can't hear you!" I say. "I'll just see you tomorrow!" and then I hang up on him, knowing that he'll keep calling – keep trying to push me out of his perfect new life. He'll keep on lying and wriggling out of things for ever.

I open the red sticker packet in my hand and there he is – Lucas Bailey, his face shining up at me, as though he's trying to tell me something.

"What should I do, Lucas?" I ask. Then the phone rings again and I know what I need to do. I don't want to be "rearranged" again. I don't want to be lied to any more.

I hold on to the sticker tightly and close my eyes. I imagine my dad and me laughing together and everything being like it used to – before he started lying. I whisper quietly, as the phone rings out, "I wish that tomorrow, just for one day, every adult in the world **had** to tell the truth."

That second the phone stops, as though my wish has silenced it. Silenced the lies he was about to tell me. When it starts again a few seconds later it makes me jump, even though I know exactly who it is. I ignore it until Mum shouts, "Answer the phone, will you?" in her nasty voice, so I switch off the phone and leave it on the side. Unless he's telling the truth, I don't want to hear it any more.

I run upstairs and update my wish list.

ARCHIE CRUMB'S WISH LIST

1. XBOX & PIZZA
2. THE BIGGEST STICKER COLLECTION IN THE WORLD
3. ICE CREAM VAN
4. REVENGE ON THE B-B GANG
5. UNICORN FOR SCADGE
6. GET PICKED FOR THE FOOTBALL TOURNAMENT
7. THE OTHER ARCHIE CRUMB
8. THE TRUTH
9.

Only one more wish left. I need to make it count.

CHAPTER EIGHTEEN

Be yourself. Everyone is unique. —Lucas Bailey

Apart from Archie Crumbs — there seems to be loads of us! —Archie Crumb

As soon as I wake up, I remember my wish and sit bolt upright.

I listen out as if I might be able to hear the chaos of the truth. I wonder what my wish will do to the world?! Does telling the truth *really* make everything better? I guess I am about to find out.

I quickly flick the telly on to a boring-looking programme, with men in suits sitting at desks discussing politics. A very dull, tired-looking man is droning on in a bored voice.

"Yes, well, the situation is escalating, no doubt,

and the question is, what should our role be? Your thoughts, Michael?"

I wait breathlessly.

"Sorry, Jeremy, I've got a very itchy bottom. It's completely distracting me and I've not actually been listening to a word you have been saying."

Jeremy almost chokes on the water he's sipping. The other suited men look completely shocked, apart from one of them, who starts laughing.

"Well, thank you for your honesty, Michael. It's now nine o'clock and time to head over to the newsroom with Debbie."

In the moments before the camera cuts to Debbie I can see the faces of the men in the studio. They can't believe what has just happened. One stands up, looking furious, the other is still laughing and Michael just sits there looking confused and scratching his bottom. Seeing his dazed expression, as though he has no idea what's happened, makes me laugh so hard. I keep picturing him saying, "I've got a very itchy bottom" over and over again and, every time I think of it, I'm laughing harder and harder. Tears start streaming down my face. I had no idea this wish was going to be so good!

When I have finally stopped laughing I decide to

see whether the honesty is working on Mum. I pop my head around Mum's door and ask, "Morning, Mum, how you feeling?"

"Terrible. I'm not going to get out of bed all day and I'm going to have a good old cry."

Well, that's honest, I think, but then Mum is always pretty honest about how bad she feels. In a way I wish she was less truthful about some things. But I can't exactly wish for that, can I?!

I pack my rucksack and jump straight on Jack. I'm really hungry but Dad always has crumpets and Shreddies at his house, so I'll eat when I get there. On my way, as I'm freewheeling down Highton Street, I realize I'm about to meet my REAL dad, the one who can't lie to me any more. I pedal a little faster. Occasionally Michael and his itchy bottom pop into my head and a wave of hysteria passes through me. I'm pretty early, so I decide that I might as well have some fun on the way.

When I see the little parade of shops coming up on Tooley Street, I slow down, park Jack up, lean him against the wall and go into the newsagent.

"Morning," the man behind the counter says as I open the door.

"Morning," I say. "How are you?"

"Tired," he says.

"Why?" I ask. "Did you have a late night?"

"No," the man says. "My wife snores. She keeps me awake every night." He blinks, as though he didn't mean to tell me this, and starts rearranging the chewing gum.

"Oh no, that sounds bad," I say, unable to hide a smile.

"She sounds like a rhinoceros," he tells me. "The neighbours complained once, that's how loud it is."

At that moment a small lady steps out of the back of the shop.

"Darling, when you've finished serving this young man could you give us a hand out back?"

"I'm not serving him, I'm just telling him about your snoring, dear."

"Malcolm!" she says sharply, and instantly goes bright red. "What on earth are you doing telling this young man about our sleeping habits!" I skulk out of the door, leaving Malcolm to clear up the mess he's got himself into.

On my way out of the shop, I bump into two ladies with small dogs.

"Be careful!" one of them snaps as I back away.

"He nearly trod on my new shoes!" says the other lady, and as I walk away, I can hear her say, "Do you like them, Yasmin, I bought them yesterday – they cost *far* too much money!"

I slow down just enough to hear Yasmin reply, "No, they are horrible, darling, possibly the ugliest shoes I've ever seen."

I have to run before the laugh that's inside me pops out too loudly. This is all just too good.

I'm nearly back at Jack when I see my dentist, Dr Maughton, coming straight towards me. I try and put my head down. It's been so long since I went to see him, there's a chance he won't recognize me, but then he calls out, "Archie Crumb!"

Oh no! I think about all of the ignored letters in the bin and missed appointments.

"Hi," I say.

"I've not seen you for a long time. How are those gnashers?"

"Good, thanks." Then I think about my truth wish and add, "How are yours? Are you looking after them?"

He looks all around us, checking that no one is near, then he leans in, whispering, "You know what, Archie, I have never told anyone this, but I am completely addicted to Haribo – had them for breakfast this morning!"

I look at him and stifle my laughter. He gives his head a little shake and says, "I have no idea why I told you that."

"Don't worry," I say, "it's only the truth!" and then I jump on Jack, still laughing, and head towards my dad's house.

As I ride my bike past a big group of joggers, I hear one of them say, "I don't even like running, I only come because I fancy Mike."

By the time I arrive at Dad and Julie's, I'm wondering how telling the truth will work out for everyone. Maybe Yasmin and her friend will have a huge argument about the ugly shoes. The jogger might tell Mike how she feels and they might live happily ever after. The newsagent might finally do something about his snoring wife, and maybe the dentist will own up to everyone about his Haribo addiction and stop telling off kids for eating sweets.

I'm about to find out the truth from my dad and I'm not entirely sure where it will take me, but there's no going back now. I start to feel my heart thumping in my chest; I'm really nervous. I take a couple of breaths in and think about what I'll say. Then the door opens before I even have time to knock.

"What are you doing out here, Arch?" Dad says. "Come in, then!"

I step inside. He looks happy to see me. Maybe he wasn't calling to cancel yesterday after all.

I go and dump my bag in the spare room and then come down to make crumpets. Scadge runs over and jumps up into my arms.

"Archibald!" she squeals. "Did you know there are three hundred and fifty-one days until my birthday?"

"No, I didn't, Scadge. You must be so excited!"

"I can't wait," she says.

Then Julie comes in with her perfectly white coat on and her pink lipstick. She brings a smell of perfume with her and I inhale deeply.

"Right, Scarlett, shoes on. We have to go."

"Where are you going?" I ask Scadge. I'm not sure if I want Julie to be honest with me, so I talk to Scadge instead.

Then Dad walks in and grabs the keys from the bowl on top of the cupboard.

"We're off out for the day, Arch. I tried to call you yesterday, to let you know, but your phone was playing up."

"OK, great. Where are we going?" I ask, leaning down to help Scadge with her zip.

"Oh, there's no need for you to come along, Arch, that's why I was trying to call. You could've just come over later. We're heading into town. It's my fault. Julie told me ages ago that she'd, er, organized something. I should have told you sooner."

I start feeling myself going red and I see Julie looking down at the floor. I know that now is my chance, but I'm starting to feel sick, realizing that this might not be such a good wish after all. The fun of the morning has suddenly completely vanished.

"Don't you want me to come?" I whisper.

"No, son, I don't. This is for me, Julie and Scarlett as a family."

He looks uncomfortable now, confused by what he just said. He turns to Julie. "You get Scarlett in the car, love, and I'll be right there." I hear Scadge saying, "Why can't Archibald come for the photos though?" as Julie bundles her out of the door.

"It's a bit complicated today, Arch. You're grown up enough to understand, so I'll be honest. Julie has booked us in for a family photo shoot. I forgot all about the damn thing until yesterday. She wants some nice piccies with Scarlett and so we thought it best if you stay here."

184

"You don't want me in the photos," I say, my stomach plummeting.

"No. Julie wanted some mother-daughter shots. She probably thinks you're a bit grubby."

"What about you?" I whisper. "What do *you* think?"

"Every time I look at you, Archie, I think about your mum," he says. "So I didn't really want you in them either."

He looks a bit defeated now, shocked and saddened by how he really feels, like maybe all the lying he does is as much for himself as for anyone else.

"You understand, don't you, Arch?" he says, in a slightly pleading voice. "Believe me, the last thing you want is to be preened and prodded by Julie all afternoon. We'll be back by tea. OK?"

I don't say anything and he heads out the door. As I watch him go, I can feel the tears prick in my eyes. I don't even know why I'm sad. I don't want to be in some stupid family photos where everyone pretends to be happy. Julie's right, I am grubby and I'm not part of this family and so I shouldn't be in them.

Then I think of Scadge saying "Cheese!" for the camera and the tears start streaming down my cheeks. I try all of my tricks but nothing stops them.

I scream, "Bananas" and even pinch my arm until it goes really numb, but the tears keep on coming. I don't know what to do with myself, but I know that I have to get out of this shiny, fake house full of lies. I can't be here any more. I can't ever let Dad make me feel this rubbish again.

Before I go, I head up to Scadge's room, tears still streaming, and find her best unicorn notepad. I take one of the pages, and with a pink pen with a pom-pom on the end I write:

Dear Scadge,
    Just so you know, it was me who got you the unicorn.
    I wish you could have kept it.
    I won't be coming over from now on.
    I'm really really sorry. If it were up to me I would see you ALL THE TIME. You are the best little sister in the whole world.
    I will miss you SO much.
    I love you.
    Archibald xxx

By the time I've finished writing I can barely breathe, sobs heaving in my lungs, the pain strong in my chest, tears hitting the paper. This is the reason I never let myself cry; it feels like I'll never stop. Everything seems even worse now than it did before the stupid wishes. I'm losing Scadge *and* Mouse, Mum is still in bed and now I really know how Dad feels about me. I thought that wishes coming true would make my life better, but it couldn't really get any worse.

I wipe my face, my chest still panting with sobs, and slowly close Scadge's door. As I grab my rucksack and go back downstairs through the pristine hall and back into the perfect kitchen, I start saying under my breath, "It's not fair", over and over, getting louder and louder with each one.

"It's not fair. It's not fair. IT'S NOT FAIR!"

Anger starts building inside me. *Why should I be shut out of this family? Why should I be so alone? Why does my life have to be so hard?* I want to mess up their perfect house. I want to show them that I'm angry and hurt and I don't want to let them get away with it.

On the cupboard is a little potted rose. I pick it up and, before I can talk myself out of it, I tip the whole thing upside down, seeing the soil hit the white rug. I feel a split second of panic but then it feels good, like I'm finally standing up for myself. I throw the fruit from the bowl all over the floor and stamp the satsumas into the ground. Then I go to the kitchen and throw the rubbish bin all over the tiles.

Then I open my rucksack and fill my bag as full as I can with sweets and biscuits, crumpets and cakes. I greedily shove in all of the things I can never afford to add to my Tesco basket. I find some shopping bags and keep filling them up. When I see a bottle of Summer Breeze fabric conditioner, I take the lid off and inhale the beautiful fresh smell and then I take it to the perfect sofa and pour the entire bottle over it. I feel like something wild has taken me over, like an animal. It makes me feel stronger, as though I've changed the feeling of pain into something else, something powerful and scary but something that no one will be able to ignore. *I'm not going to let them get away with treating me like this*, I think as I throw the empty bottle across the room. I turn and look at the mess I've made and then close the door behind me. Out on the pavement outside I get Lucas out of my pocket and shout loud into the sky,

"I am NEVER EVER making another wish EVER again."

CHAPTER NINETEEN

The time is right to be the person you have always wanted to be. —Lucas Bailey

The time is right to pretend I didn't do the really bad thing that I just did. —Archie Crumb

I don't tell anyone about what I did, not even Mouse. I make sure the phone is switched off when I get home and I decide to ignore the door if anyone knocks. Mum never answers it anyway.

I wait for them to come for the whole of Saturday night, with a stern knock and an angry look on their faces, but they don't. I imagine Julie crying and screaming about her white rug. I imagine the arguments and anger, deciding what should be done.

By the time I go to bed, though, I realize that nothing will be done. They will tidy up and get on with their perfect life and feel pleased and relieved every other weekend when I don't show up. This is exactly what they wanted.

On Sunday, when I go round for tea, Mouse knows that something's wrong, but she presumes it's because of the house move. I let her think that and talk about our plan and the viewings. It kind of distracts me from thinking about Dad and Julie, and as we sit watching the match, making some more realistic spiders, I think that maybe I'll be fine without them. I just need to make sure I don't lose Mouse.

We carry on with our plan to scare off the house viewers. It works perfectly for the next two viewings. The couples hurry out through the front door looking terrified.

But on Tuesday, things start falling apart.

The first viewing arrives. I do my bit and tell them all about a local gang of kids who have started a street fighting club, which meets every Friday night right outside the house. They go in looking anxious and some time passes – and then Mouse comes out looking like she's been crying and I know something's gone wrong.

"They caught me," she says. "Mum and Dad came into my room and found the kipper."

"Oh no!"

"It's over," she says. "We may as well give up, Archie. I'm moving away and that's that."

"NO!" I shout. "I won't let it happen. *You* can't do anything, but that doesn't stop me from trying."

"OK, but be careful. Meet at the betting shop later?"

I intercept the little old couple who arrive for the next viewing and tell them about all-night house parties next door, and they look pretty freaked out when they walk towards the house. I rub my hands together, knowing that my work is done.

An hour later as I'm waiting for my final victims of the day, a policeman walks down the road at the same time that a couple get out of their car and look up at the house with big smiles on their faces. Just as I make my move towards them the policeman passes me and says, "You all right, son?"

"Yeah," I say, trying to sound casual but desperate for him to keep walking so that I can talk to the man and woman, who are now heading towards the front door.

That's when it all goes wrong. The policeman nods

at the couple and they stop and ask him a question which ruins everything that I'm about to tell them.

"Hello, officer," says the man. "We're looking at moving to the area. What's it like around here?"

"Is it safe, officer?" adds the woman.

"Call me Rob, I'm off-duty," he says. I try to stop myself from laughing. Imagine being called Rob and being a policeman! Then he carries on talking and I soon stop smiling.

"You won't get a better road than this one. I've never had a single call out to this street. It's not the fanciest area, but I tell you what, it's as safe as they come."

"The neighbours are weirdos!" I shout abruptly, pointing to Mr and Mrs Stanley's. They all turn to me, confusion on their faces, and at the very same moment the door to Mr and Mrs Stanley's house opens and they come out with a tray of delicious-looking buns.

"Archie, we've seen you out here all afternoon – you must be starving. Have a bun. Help yourself, officer." I see the policeman taking two of the biggest buns on the plate. "And you must be looking at next door – help yourselves." I put my head into my hands as the Stanleys start telling the couple all about the neighbourhood and they all laugh and eat the stupid cakes.

Rob, the policeman with the funny name, steps over to me.

"I'm going to take a guess," he whispers in between mouthfuls of cake, "that for some reason you don't want this house to be sold. Am I right?"

I nod miserably as I watch the couple wave to Mr and Mrs Stanley and go into Mouse's house, looking just like two people about to buy their new home.

"Is it your house and you don't want to move, or your friend's and you don't want them to go?"

"My friend," I say.

"And I came along and ruined your plan?" he asks. I think Rob must be a pretty good policeman if he has figured all this out so easily.

I nod.

"Ah, that's tough, buddy. I'm sorry. I had to tell them the truth, you know. If I gave you my other bun, would that help?"

I shake my head.

Later on, as I'm sitting on the wall staring vacantly into the betting shop, I look down the road to see if Mouse is coming and instead see Julie jogging towards me in her pink Lycra.

I immediately get up and start walking quickly away from her, hoping that she hasn't seen me, or if she has, that she doesn't want to see me just as much as I don't want to see her. I've been trying to forget what I did to their house. I kind of imagined that it would just go away. That I would never see them again and that would be it. That I could try and forget how painful it all feels. I put my hood up and walk as quickly as I can for a few blocks and when I turn around to check that she's gone I can see her waving and shouting, "Archie! Stop!"

I can't stop. I can't look her in the eyes. I break into a run but she just keeps on following and shouting. We run for what feels like miles. My heart is racing and my chest is burning – I'm not a very good runner. Eventually, when I can't go any further, I stop and collapse, panting with my hands on my thighs. Julie runs up behind me and then stops and does the same.

"Wow, not bad, Archie," she says between breaths. "I didn't think you were ever going to stop!"

When we have finally got our breath back, awkwardness floods through my body and I feel terrible. I don't know if I should start running again or apologize for everything.

"Why did you follow me?" I pant.

"I ran this way hoping to see you. I've been running this way since Saturday but you've not been around."

"I've been helping a friend," I say, thinking of Mouse and how she might be at the wall, wondering where on earth I am.

"Archie, about what happened."

"I'm sorry I wrecked your house," I say, looking at the ground.

"No, *I'm* sorry, Archie."

I look up. "What for?"

"Everything. Leaving you out of the pictures, the caravan, cancelling your visits – everything."

I take a deep breath and just say it. "Why do you hate me so much?"

"I don't hate you, Archie! Of course I don't. I was just nervous – scared, I suppose. I have no idea how to be around you. It's a bit weird being a stepmum. I don't know how to do it right. You may have noticed that I'm a bit of a perfectionist?"

"Maybe I noticed that a little bit," I say, smiling at the thought of her pristine white carpets.

She smiles back at me, a little sadly. "I was so worried about getting it wrong, I stopped trying. Tried to keep you separate. I thought things would be ... easier that way. It's not fair though, and it took you trashing my house to see that."

"What about Dad?"

"Your dad loves you very much," she says. "He's not always great at expressing his feelings. He's been trying to call you every day..."

"I don't want to talk to him," I say.

She nods. "Well, that's between you both. I just wanted to say sorry – without your dad being involved. Scarlett – Scadge – really loves you too, you know."

"I love her too. She's the funniest person I know."

"She really is." We stand there for a while in silence, and just when I think that Julie's about to do the sigh/laugh she says, "The other day she was trying to turn the bin into a unicorn and fell in when she tried to ride it!"

"Remember when *you* fell in the unicorn poo in the garden?!" I say, giggling at the memory of her sliding around angrily in the poo.

"Oh god, don't remind me! That skirt was ruined!" she says, trying not to laugh.

"You were so furious."

"There was a pooping pony in my garden!"

"Actually, I think if you ask Scadge, you will find

it was a unicorn!"

"Magical Mystical Sparkles the Third!" we both say in unison.

After a pause, she says gently, "You and your dad will sort things out."

I'm not so sure we will, but I don't tell her that. All I know is that I'm never going to let him make me cry like that again.

"I'd better get back to the wall. I was meant to be meeting my friend, and she'll be wondering where I am." And we head back towards the betting shop, telling stories about Scadge and her unicorn adventures. It's the first time that it feels normal between me and Julie, the first time that she doesn't do the laugh/sigh. Maybe she's not so bad after all.

I wave to Julie as she jogs off and head over to the wall and Mouse. The minute I see her and Flump, sitting dejectedly, I know that the house viewing has gone far too well. "They loved it," she sniffs. "They even loved the turquoise bath. NO ONE loves the turquoise bath. What did you say to them? It really didn't work."

I tell her about the policeman and the buns.

"No wonder they loved it," she says, when I've finished. "It sounds like a scene from an old film!

The friendly neighbourhood policeman and perfect neighbours! What are we going to do, Arch?" Then, after a pause: "Do you think it's time to risk it and make a wish?"

"I can't. It's too dangerous," I say, thinking about what happened at Dad's house, my wish backfiring in such a painful way. "If I wished for you to not move house you might end up stuck there for the rest of your life. Or if I wished for the people who love the turquoise bath to take away their offer then another person would just offer the next day. We can't control everything. I've realized I just need to find a way to make things happen for myself rather than trusting some stupid wishes."

Mouse nods sadly. She gets it.

"I guess I'm moving to the country, then." She rests her head on my shoulder, and we both stare into the lights of the betting shop.

CHAPTER TWENTY

The opinions of others don't define you.
—Lucas Bailey

Opinions are like bums: we've all got one!
—Archie Crumb

When I get home, Rosemary's at our front door.

"Oh, Archie, I've been knocking. Is your mum not in?"

"No," I lie. "She's gone out."

"OK, love. How are you?" She looks like she really means it. Not like the usual empty "How are you". Imagine if every time someone asked, you actually told them the truth.

"Well, I've got a blister on my big toe because my shoes are rubbing and all of the water is leaking through the bottom so my socks are wet. Oh, yes, and my dad's a liar and I have decided not to see him any more and my mum has basically been living in bed for the last year. How are you?!"

The nicest person in the world might not know how to deal with all that.

No, in my experience it's best to nod and say, "Fine, thanks," which is exactly what I'm about to say to Rosemary, but when I open my mouth I think about how I'll be lying, just like my dad. Lying about what's really happening. Always lying. To teachers, to Mouse and Zoe, to Rosemary and maybe to myself.

But the truth is dangerous too – I should know. How are you meant to know when it's right to tell the truth? When it's OK to ask for help?

Rosemary bends down a little bit so she can look me in the eye.

"We're a little worried about you, Archie," she says. "James said your mum was ill. I've not seen her in months."

I'm so close to saying something, to telling her what's really happening, but then I remember Mum saying not to tell anyone and I whisper, "We're fine. She was ill and now she's busy. Anyway, I'd better go, I've got homework to do. Bye."

I unlock the door fast and shut it behind me, my heart thumping. I can't believe I nearly slipped up and told Rosemary. I don't know what's wrong with me. Mum would be so angry. She just needs a bit more time, I know that.

I run upstairs and poke my head around her door. "Hi, Mum."

"Hello, sweetie. How was your day?"

"OK," I say, half wondering if I should tell her about Mouse leaving. I don't want to think about that right now, so I tell her about Rosemary instead.

"She was asking how you were," I say as I sit on the end of the bed.

"What did you say, honey?"

"Just that you were busy, but she said she was worried about us."

"Nosy old boot."

"No, she's nice, Mum, honest. She let me use her toilet the other day."

"I don't want her poking her nose into our business, Archie. We're doing fine, aren't we? I'm on the way up, I can feel it."

"I'm a sub in a football tournament in a couple of weeks," I say, changing the subject. "We are playing at Valley Stadium. It should be great. Lucas Bailey's going to be there and everything!"

"That's brilliant, sweetie," she says, but I can tell that she's not really listening. Her brain has already spiralled off towards her illness so I just get up and tell her I have homework to do.

"Shall I bring you some dinner up in a bit?" I say.

"Thanks, sweetie. I'm sorry that I'm so useless."

I dash out of the room before I'm trapped by her sadness.

School is actually not so bad now that me and Mouse are friends again. At break we sit on the wall and sell stickers. I'm earning quite a bit of pocket money. Mr Fell is making us train every lunchtime so I can only sell them at break. He says that we need to "be at the top of our game".

Because I'm the sub I just sit and watch, which I'm pretty used to. I shout inspirational quotes and tell them how well they are doing. Mr Fell says that I'm a "good motivator" and even asks me to give the team talk before we start training each day. I always just say some more of the quotes from the stickers, but everyone seems to listen. It feels good, like I'm helping.

Today, Mouse is sitting with me.

"The couple who loved the turquoise bath put in

an offer yesterday," she says.

"Does that mean that you're definitely leaving?" I ask.

"Yeah, they want to move quickly so it looks like we'll be gone in a few weeks. I can't even come to watch the tournament as we are going to look at houses that weekend."

She looks so sad, and I feel terrible. I want to do something to help.

"Do you want me to use my last wish?" I ask.

"I thought you'd given up?"

"I have. My wish about always being told the truth scared me, but if you want me to then I will."

Mouse glances at me. "What if you wished for us to be friends for ever instead?"

"We don't need a wish for that. We can definitely make that happen ourselves ... wherever you live."

"In that case, who needs wishes? You are pretty wise, Archie Crumb, you know that?"

Even though I know that she's leaving, in this moment – sitting next to my best friend, cheering on my very own football team and feeling the sun on my skin – I feel fine. In this moment there is nothing that I would change. I wouldn't wish for anything else.

When the team has finished training, Mr Fell gathers us all around and hands out letters.

"Right, lads, tickets. You'll obviously have loads of family and friends who want to come and see you play in one of the biggest stadiums in the country. As you're on the team, you get discounted tickets. All the money goes to charity and you can get tickets on the day, but they are more expensive, so I suggest you go on the website. I want to fill the stand with the best supporters ever. We want banners, drums, costumes, the lot."

When I look down at the letter, I see that each ticket is £20! There's no way Mum could afford that. It's a good job that she won't want to come anyway. I'm glad I'm just a sub; I wouldn't want to be on that huge pitch with no one to cheer for me. I don't even let myself think about Dad and Scadge and how much she would love to come and cheer me on. I put the letter in the bin on my way back to class.

CHAPTER TWENTY-ONE

You always have the opportunity to change
yourself. —Lucas Bailey

I wish I could change these trousers; they're
far too tight. —Archie Crumb

The next week seems to go into double time. I'm
training every day (watching and cheering as the
others train most of the time) and me and Mouse are
going through all of her stuff in her bedroom after
school. Her mum and dad said that they are doing
a huge clear-out before the move, so we spend every
day in her room drinking juice and eating biscuits
while I hold up teddies and books and she says yes
or no. Then I throw the teddy or T-shirt or whatever
I'm holding on to the correct pile – Keep or Go. She

says that I can have anything on the Go pile. So far, I've got a huge pile of books, two football shirts and a load of games.

Flump is nestling on my knee. I hold up an empty money box in the shape of an elephant. Mouse says, "No," and I put it on the Go pile.

"Maybe I should take this, actually," I say. "I'm earning quite a lot from sticker sales. I need somewhere to put it all!"

It's a big business now, sticker selling. Kids all know where to find me. I do five packs for a pound, which is way cheaper than the shops. Jayden Thomas bought twenty-five packs off me and then tried to sell them on for more. He was asking people to pay a pound for three packs, which obviously no one did, apart from Felix Ratton, but only because Jayden had him in a headlock. That's no way to do business, if you ask me. I've never seen a shopkeeper putting someone in a headlock to force them to buy a loaf of bread.

I have to be careful now not to get caught selling, as Mrs Mather found out and had a talk with the whole class about "illegal trading on school property", which made it sound way worse than it is. So I make sure that it looks like we're just chatting on the wall and I slip the stickers into people's pockets and ask them to leave the money on the wall. I was trying to do that cool thing with handshakes, where you shake someone's hand and slip the money/stickers over with no one noticing, but it kept going wrong. Hayden Phillips called me a weirdo and Dan Dore dropped two pounds all in coppers and they jangled and rolled everywhere.

"What are you going to spend your illegal earnings on?" Mouse asks.

"No idea. I used to spend any money I had on stickers, but there's no point in that any more. I might get Mum a present."

We carry on sorting the piles and as we get to Mouse's lucky football shirt she holds it up and smiles.

"Did you see the school website yet?" she asks.

"No, why?"

"My speech is on it." I stop what I'm doing and look at her.

"Miss Crowther filmed it on her iPad."

"I thought she wasn't even watching."

"Me too. She said it was one of the best speeches on feminism that she had ever heard and that the whole school community should see it. Just a shame it was too late for the tournament. Although that doesn't really matter now I can't go anyway. At least people will see it. Maybe it will change things next time and they will think about how to let girls join in a bit more."

"That's so cool, Mouse. I told you, no one can *ever* ignore you. You just have to keep on telling people what you think. I wish I could be more like that."

"You know, Archie," she says as she folds the football shirt and puts it in the Keep pile, "I was thinking. There's one thing that I'd love you to have. I know you get lonely and I'd like you to have a reminder of me."

"I've got a huge pile of reminders," I say, pointing to my pile of stuff.

"Books and toys can't keep you company though, can they? I want you to have a friend." She pauses and takes a breath in. "I want you to have Flump."

"You can't give me Flump! She's your favourite." I look down at Flump's white fur and give her a stroke.

"She's your favourite too and she loves you. If you have Flump it's a bit like I'm still here." I stroke Flump's soft little body and force down the sad feeling in my chest.

"Well, you're not going anywhere just yet, so let's

wait and see," I say, holding Flump a little tighter.

On Saturday it's the last day of training before the tournament. Mr Fell gathers us all together.

"Right, lads, we're nearly there. I just wanted to let you all know that I'm proud of how hard you've been working, and I'll be proud no matter how well we do. As you may know, Henry Bude's sick and won't be playing tomorrow and so I have drafted in Archie Crumb."

I look up, terrified, but see the other Archie standing next to Mr Fell, grinning. The others all say, "Yes!" under their breath and pump their fists. They all know how good Archie is.

Mr Fell carries on: "So we have a really strong team and can keep our wonderful subs on the bench if we need some fresh legs tomorrow."

Jayden Thomas looks at me and whispers, "Bad luck, Crumby!"

Mr Fell continues, "I got an email this morning from the ground. There'll be a television crew at the stadium and it will be shown live on the BBC."

When he says this, I'm relieved I'm not actually playing. The last thing I would want is my terrible lack of skills to be caught on camera for the world to laugh at.

Then he says, "So let's just have a good last session and go in tomorrow positive and together. It's going to be quite an experience. Now, Archie, could we have some of your words of wisdom, to keep us going until tomorrow?" I think about the last sticker packet I sold and remember the quote on the back.

"Your only limitation is your imagination," I say, then I carry on, this time using my own words. "If you can't imagine us winning tomorrow then we have no chance, so close your eyes and picture us holding up that trophy." I look at them and they are actually doing it, so I keep going. "Imagine scoring that winning goal and, when you can see it clearly, then you need to start believing it can happen. I believe it can. To be honest after the few weeks I've had, I believe that *anything's* possible! Come on, Valleybrook, WE CAN DO THIS!" They all start cheering and slapping each other on the back.

"Nice one, Archie," says the other Archie Crumb, smiling down at me.

As we all start warming up and stretching, I take a look around me at all of the kids who I barely speak to. Maybe I should try a bit harder now that Mouse is leaving. I've never tried to make other friends, as I've always had her. I just assume that no one wants to hang out with me, but maybe that's not true. Maybe it's just something that I imagined and so I made it true. I look at Dan Dore and think about all the times he's asked me to play at lunchtime, even when no one else really wanted me to. As we are running on the spot, touching our knees, I say, "You looking forward to tomorrow?"

"Yeah," he says. "You?"

"Yeah, I can't wait to see Lucas Bailey."

"Me neither. My whole family are coming, they've made a massive banner."

I smile and keep lifting my knees up.

"And it's on the telly too – so they can watch it again and again!" I say.

"I know! My mum's baked a cake in the shape of a football for after. She's completely bonkers."

When we're finished warming up, I head towards the bench and watch them as they start taking penalties at Milan Finch, the goalkeeper. He's so good, not scared at all. Every time the ball heads towards the net it's like he knows exactly which way to leap, a bit like I did when the magic of the wish kicked in, but he's like that all the time. Totally in the moment.

Just as Dan steps up to take his penalty I feel a sharp, cold breeze on the back of my neck and it makes me shudder. Something suddenly doesn't feel right, like something's about to happen.

I think back to my wish, trying to remember my words. I wished to *be in the tournament*. I didn't wish to be sitting on the bench, cheering people on and saying inspirational quotes, did I? I start to panic. Maybe my wish is not completely over yet.

I see Dan strike the ball high into the air and Milan hurl himself at full stretch across the front of the goal, his fingers just grazing the ball as it flies into the back of the net, and then his body twists in the air as he comes down towards the ground. I can see it before it happens. His left arm lands hard on the ground underneath his body and everyone can hear the sound.

CRACK.

His face says it all. His arm's broken. The day before the tournament.

"NO!" I shout as everyone crowds around the net and Mr Fell tells them to back away.

Two hours later, after Milan has been X-rayed, Mr Fell calls us all together before the end of training.

"Right, lads, it's bad news, I'm afraid. Milan has broken his wrist and won't be able to play tomorrow. The good news is we have a fantastic sub, don't we, Archie?" I hear a low groan coming from some of the other kids.

"Enough of that, lads. Archie earned his place on the team just like you all did. He made a fantastic save in the trials and I'm sure he'll make some equally fantastic saves tomorrow. I hope you've got people coming to watch you, Arch? It's going to be a pretty big day!"

I swallow. "Sir, I'm not sure that I'm the best..."

"Nonsense, Archie. You're bound to be nervous, but you're part of this team for a reason. Now you can cheer them on from the pitch rather than the sidelines. Your enthusiasm makes a real difference, don't forget it."

Maybe I should wish to go back in time, I think wildly, *and undo all my wishes*. But then I think back on the last few weeks. Sitting in the ice cream van with Mouse, running downstairs to find the box full of stuff, seeing Scadge's face as I lifted her on to the uni-pony, my room full of stickers and seeing Dad for what he really is. Even though wishing has been tough, it has made my life a lot more interesting. I'm not sure that I would want to take them all back, however badly they turned out.

That night at Mouse's, as we are putting all of my stuff from the Go pile into a big box, I tell her about Milan and the CRACK.

"So I'm in goal," I say quietly, knowing how much she wanted to be on the team. But she doesn't seem upset at all.

"I can't believe I won't see you, Archie! Will your mum go?"

"No," I say. "It's probably for the best, I'll just embarrass myself."

"If you go into it thinking that, then you definitely will. You need to believe in yourself. I've heard you giving your team talks, but it's no good if you don't believe it yourself."

This makes me think of Mum and how maybe I'm doing the same thing as she is. Saying all the right things but nothing really changing. Then I remember the truth of the situation.

"But I'm terrible at football," I say. "It's a fact."

"Admittedly, you are not the best, BUT you only make yourself worse by telling yourself that again and again. If you believe you can then maybe you will. If you don't wish for it then it can't come true, can it?"

"Don't talk to me about wishing, Mouse – you know where that's got me!"

As I'm walking home with my huge box of stuff, I start thinking about what Mouse said and what I told the rest of the team. If you believe that something can happen, does it make it more likely? I start imagining my mum sitting in the football stadium, watching me and clapping her hands above her head. I imagine me saving a goal and the rest of the team raising me up above their heads. I picture Scadge and Dad holding a big banner saying, GO, ARCHIE! GO! and I picture Mouse scoring the winning goal.

I know all of these things can't come true, but picturing them makes me feel so good. Maybe that's reason enough to wish or hope, just because it makes you feel good while you're doing it. Even if a wish isn't what you'd imagined or things just don't come true, perhaps you should never stop trying. Never stop dreaming of what you want. So, I stagger home behind my box and keep the image of the stadium full of people I know, all chanting my name, firmly fixed in my head, and it almost feels real.

"You are taking up the whole pavement, Crumby." Bella peers at me as I lower the box and move to the side. I've not seen her on my street before and I've never seen her when we are both on our own. I don't know if it feels safer or more dangerous. As she passes me I notice that she's wearing a hoodie that says Valley Gymnastics.

"Have you been to gymnastics again?" I ask

hopefully, remembering how horrible her dad was.

"Yeah. So?" she says uncertainly, scowling.

"I'm just happy that you went."

"You are so weird, Crumby," she says as she walks on. I remember her lonely face in the car and call after her.

"I saw your dad laughing at you."

She stops dead and I can see her breathing. "I think you should keep going to gymnastics and show him that there is nothing to laugh at." She turns and looks right at me. In the silence I know that she's making a decision, whether to stay strong and destroy me or whether to tell the truth. She takes a big breath in and decides on the truth.

"The problem is, Crumby, he's right. I'm rubbish."

"Of course you are. You only just started. Anyway, you can still enjoy something even if you are rubbish at it. Look at me and football."

"Oh god, I don't think I'm as bad as that!" We both chuckle, then she catches herself, scowls again and starts to head off. I risk one more question.

"Do you think that you and Bea will make up?"

"I doubt it," she says.

"You know Mouse is moving house?"

She shrugs and shakes her head.

"You and Bea have been friends for as long as me and Mouse have. I remember you always having your hair the same in reception – those massive blue ribbons."

"Jo Jo Bows," she says with a smile.

"It's none of my business, but I know what it's like to lose a best friend, and if there was anything that I could do to stop it I would. *You* can do something."

"Maybe. . ." she says, and then she shakes her head, and it's as though a spell has been lifted. "Anyway, it is none of your business. I've got to go. I don't want anyone to see us and think we're friends." She takes off down the road but then turns back, walking backwards and looking at me intently as she goes. Then she does a pretty terrible cartwheel, raises both her arms in the air and shouts, "Thanks, Archie!"

CHAPTER TWENTY-TWO

Everything you do, do it with a lot of love.
—Lucas Bailey

Once I made Mum's toast into a heart
shape. I covered the burned bit with jam.
—Archie Crumb

Mum's in the kitchen when I get in.

"Hello, sweetie, how was your day?" She seems different, brighter somehow, and I half wonder if this is it. Maybe she's finally getting better. As I look at her sitting at the little kitchen table in her dressing gown smiling up at me, I feel the hope and decide not to push it down, to enjoy the idea that she may be turning a corner. Even if it is just for today.

"You look good, Mum!"

"What? This old thing!" she says, swooshing her dressing gown, and we both laugh.

"I'm on the team for the tournament tomorrow!" I say. "Milan broke his arm and so I'm in goal!"

"That's brilliant! Not for poor old Milan obviously. What tournament is this?"

"I told you, Mum, the one at Valley Stadium. The one with Lucas Bailey and a TV crew and a crowd of thousands! It's going to be live on telly!"

"Oh my gosh, well, that does sound exciting. I think this deserves a celebration! Shall we have some spaghetti hoops?"

"Yes!" I say, feeling like this day really could not get any better. Maybe hoping is not such a bad thing after all.

"If it's live on TV then I can watch you, can't I? After tea you can bring the telly back downstairs," she says as she opens the tin. A tiny part of me deflates. I would love her to be there in the crowd, to leave the house and show up for me.

"You could come to the stadium," I whisper. "Everyone else has loads of family going to cheer them on."

There is a pause, and I hear her sigh as she puts the bowl into the microwave. My chest tightens in readiness for her answer.

"Archie, I would love to, but I'm just not up to it. Not right now."

I nod and sit down at the table but, in the silence, something shifts inside me. Maybe it's everything that's happened to me, all the wishing, losing Mouse and finally standing up to Dad. For once I don't want to just go along with everything Mum says and feel bad for wanting more.

"When then, Mum?" I hear myself say. "If you're not well enough to support me now and you've not been well enough for the last year, when will you be up for it? When will I have someone cheering me on again?"

"You just don't understand, Archie," she says. "You don't know what it's like for me."

"And *you* don't know what it's like for *me*!" I shout, much louder than I mean to. Much louder than I have ever shouted at Mum before. "Do you ever think about what it feels like for me? Watching you sleep all the time. Lying to everyone, telling them that you're OK when you're not. Well, I'm not OK either. None of this is OK, Mum. Not any more." I look at her and wait, almost about to take it all back, say sorry, but I don't let myself. I still have too much anger flowing through me.

There is a silence. Then she shakes her head. "I'm too tired for this, Archie." She sighs.

"Well, just go back to bed," I mumble. "I'll just look after myself like I usually do."

She looks like she might be about to speak, but then she stops herself. The microwave pings. She climbs slowly up the stairs.

After eating my spaghetti hoops on my own, I'm at the sink squidging the suds out of the sponge. I start to think that maybe there's a tiny chance she might change her mind. That she might come back downstairs and say sorry. Say that she will try her best to make it tomorrow. That she understands how hard it must be not having anyone there. I look at the door and listen for sounds of movement, but there's nothing.

What if she wakes up in the morning and feels just about well enough to come after all? I want to make it possible – just in case. I dash up the stairs and tip out my sticker money from the elephant money box. As well as using it to buy apples and broccoli, I was going to use the money to save up for Christmas, buy Mum some of her favourite perfume. I was going to get Mouse a shiny red-and-gold gerbil costume for Flump, to make her look like a superhero, but I think that this is a better thing to spend it on. And anyway, I have thousands of stickers, so I can still save for the presents. I tip out the coins and start counting. Twenty pounds exactly; it's almost like a sign.

I sneak Mum's phone out while she pretends to sleep and go on the website to look for tickets. When I get to the checkout, I realize that I can't use my money, as it's in cash. I need a card. I can't ask Mum or it will send her into a right spin; she'll start telling me there's no point buying a ticket and how sorry she is. I know her card details anyway, I use them for the Tesco shop. I've not done the shop for next week yet so I know there'll be enough in the account. Maybe if I use the card and then do half of the food shopping down at the Co-op with my cash (they do good deals on noodles anyway) then she'll never know and we won't starve. Perfect.

I check out and then realize that I need to print the ticket out. It feels like I'm on a secret mission and at each stage there is a new problem to solve. We don't have a printer, which is so annoying. I decide to head back to Mouse's and see if I can print it there.

As I'm closing the front door, I see Rosemary's head poke out of hers.

"Hello, Archie," she says, as though she's been waiting for me.

"Hi, Rosemary. Just going to get something printed at my friend's house."

"Do that here if you want? You can come in and have a juice too." Then her little dog runs out and starts jumping up at my legs, licking my hands as I bend down.

"Sir Lancelot wants to see you too, by the looks of it!" she says.

I hear my mum in my head telling me to say no and that she's being nosy, but then I look up at her kind face and think, what harm can it do? She's just being nice, and last time she gave me really nice biscuits.

As I sit on her soft sofa next to Sir Lancelot, my socked feet squishing into the thick cream carpet, she brings out a plate of custard creams and some juice.

"I miss not having James here to look after," she sighs. "It's quite lonely here on my own."

"Does James not have a dad either?" I ask, and instantly regret the word *either*, as though I've erased my dad from my story.

"He died, lovey, ten years back. It was very difficult for James, and me, but we just about coped, the two of us."

"Sorry," I mumble.

"It's all right, love. I know how difficult it can be doing it all on your own. How's your mum doing? I've still not seen her."

"She's OK," I say. "She just made tea."

"Lovely, what did you have?"

"Spaghetti hoops."

"Ooh, James used to love them. I think he probably still does! I don't think students are that good at cooking! What else does she cook for you, Archie?"

"Not much else really," I say, and I see her look a bit worried, so I add, "Rice and vegetables and fish and stuff."

We sit there quietly for a bit, and then she says, "It's OK, Archie. I know that she's struggled since your dad left. She hasn't been getting out much, has she?"

"No." I sigh and sip my juice, and then it just comes out. "She's been pretty sad, for a long time," I say, feeling my checks burning, immediately wondering if I shouldn't have said anything.

"I bet that's hard for you, having to look after her?" Rosemary says gently.

"Kind of. It's just normal now, and she says that I'm better at cooking and cleaning than most eleven-year-olds, so I guess that's kind of a good thing."

"Of course, you will have skills that other kids won't have a clue about. But you know you don't have to do it all on your own?"

"Well, Dad's not really bothered..." I start to say. "And Mum doesn't want friends to know."

Rosemary shakes her head. "I don't mean that, sweetie. There are people who could check in and help with the shopping and stuff, make sure you're OK."

"Are there?!" I say, not quite believing her.

She nods. "If you're looking after your mum, then you are what's called a *young carer*. There are groups out there that try and support young carers like you."

"I don't think Mum would really want anyone else helping," I say, suddenly feeling like I shouldn't be here, that I shouldn't be saying all of this. That's when I remember the ticket. "Can I use the printer, Rosemary?"

She sits back and nods. "Yes, of course, love."

As I am leaving with my printout, she says, "I know it feels like a big deal asking for help, but if you don't want to talk to anyone else then you can always come here for a bicky and a chat. Sir Lancelot seems very happy with the cuddles."

"Thanks, Rosemary," I say.

Knowing that I've told someone the truth and nothing bad happened feels good, like a relief. When she found out Mum was in bed, she didn't freak out or call the police or say what a bad person Mum was. She just listened.

Maybe it's not such a bad thing to tell people what's really going on.

Back in our cold kitchen with the ticket in my hand, I find a piece of paper and write a note.

Dear Mum,
    Sorry I shouted at you.
    I got you a ticket for the tournament, just in case.
    Wish me luck!!
    Archie Xxx

I'm leaving early in the morning, before she'll be up, so I sneak in and pop it by her bed. I look up to the ceiling and have to force myself not to make the wish.

No more wishing, Archie Crumb. Just hoping for

now, hoping and doing, I think. Then I remember Mum's phone. I go and get it, and as I am bringing it back to her room, I stop and quietly sit at the top of the stairs.

I click on Google and type, YOUNG CARER.

CHAPTER TWENTY-THREE

Stay positive. Stay steady. Stay strong.
—Lucas Bailey

Stay awake. Sit up. Don't fart.
—Archie Crumb

My alarm jolts me from my dream and I sit straight up in bed.

"This is it, Lucas!" I say to the sticker that's propped up by the clock. "I get to see you in real life!" I jump out of bed, grab my kit and Mouse's old football boots and head downstairs. I pour the last of the cornflakes out of the packet and finish them before the milk has even touched the bottom of the bowl, then I'm out of the door.

"Bye, Mum!" I call, knowing that she won't hear

me. "Come and see me play," I add in a whisper. "Please come and see me."

The air is cold, and I can see my breath in front of me. Dragon breath, Scadge calls it. I miss Scadge so much. She's probably taller. Maybe she hasn't even noticed that I've not been there. I shake my head, trying to ignore any bad feelings. Only the good ones are allowed in today.

As I'm heading towards the ground, I hear footsteps behind me and then:

"KARGHH KARGHHH!"

I turn to see Mouse running full pelt down the hill towards me.

"What are you doing?" I ask. "I thought you were seeing houses today."

"I am," pants Mouse. "But I wanted to say good luck!" And she grabs me into a huge hug. "If I get back in time then I'll meet you at the ground after – deal?"

"Deal. Good luck with the house-hunting," I call after her as she runs back up the hill.

By the time I find our meeting point outside the ground, I'm super excited. I can't stop jiggling and jumping around, knowing that Lucas Bailey and so many other faces from my stickers are about to become real. I keep focused on that, as every time I think about actually trying to save a goal, I feel sick.

There are coaches full of teams from other schools all arriving and lining up. Some of the kids look massive, like a team full of giants rather than eleven-year-olds.

"I hope we don't have to play *them*," Dan Dore whispers as he points towards a terrifying team in green-and-white stripes who look like they've all just come out of a boxing ring. There are scars and bruises all over their huge bodies.

"Yeah, me too!" I giggle nervously. Everyone seems as excited as me and I really feel like I'm part of the team. The other Archie Crumb even puts his arm around my shoulders as we head into the stadium and says, "Big respect for doing this, Archie. It's not easy coming on as a sub."

"Thanks, Archie," I say. "You too."

The organizers gather us all together on the pitch and it feels unbelievable. The size of the stadium. The rows and rows of empty seats which, in a matter of hours, will be filled with noise and banners. It almost makes me go dizzy when I look out into it. At least if Mum doesn't show up, I won't even notice. There's no way you could find anyone in a crowd this size.

A man in a hat, with a big bunch of keys dangling from his belt, starts tapping at a microphone, making popping sounds over the speakers until we're all quiet.

"Welcome to the tournament, folks." There is a ripple of excitement and whispering. "There's a list of matches on the board. Each team will play eight ten-minute matches until we are left with our quarter-finalists. We will then move on to the semi-finals after lunch and will narrow down to our two final teams for the big match at the end of the day, which will be watched by the current Valley squad, including, of course, the organizer of this tournament, Lucas Bailey." Kids start whooping and cheering when he says this.

"There'll also be a skills demonstration by the Valley squad, which I, for one, am really looking forward to. You have an hour to warm up and familiarize yourselves with the ground before the doors to the public are opened. Good luck, everyone."

We have an area that's just for our team. It has a flag with the school crest of a four-leaf clover on it so that we know where to go if we get lost. Me, Dan and the other Archie head to the toilets. On the way we pass loads of food places opening their shutters and security people speaking into walkie-talkies. I've never been anywhere like this – it's huge. It feels like something out of a movie or from the future. Dan can tell that I'm taking it all in for the first time, from the look on my face,

"It's pretty cool, isn't it?" he asks, and I nod. "Have you ever seen them play?"

"Only on the telly," I say. "Have you?"

"Yeah, my dad's got a season ticket so I come all the time. I'm not really as into it as him, I like playing more than watching, but Mum says it makes him happy so I keep coming with him."

"Yeah," I say, laughing as if I have any idea what he's talking about. I can't imagine what it must be like having a dad who wants to spend time with you. I think back to being little, sitting on Dad's knee as he watched the World Cup. Being thrown into the air when England scored. I'm about to play in one of the biggest football stadiums in the country and he doesn't even know that I'm here.

By the time we find the loos and make our way back to the four-leaf clover, it's time to warm up. The pitch has been divided with chalk into three smaller pitches so that lots of games can happen at once. We are shown where to warm up and sir tells us to stretch, and then he does some quick games with us, making us jump when he shouts, "One!" and touch the ground when he shouts, "Two!"

After that he throws a ball to Jayden Thomas and tells everyone to line up for a shot at goal. My heart sinks. I'd kind of been ignoring this reality, hoping that I would somehow get away with it. Not have to show everyone just how bad I am. Every single shot goes past me and with each one I can feel myself getting redder and redder. I look over to sir and can see a slight look of panic creeping into his face. Luckily, I'm rescued by a loud whistle and the man with the jangly bunch of keys starts tapping the microphone again.

"The doors are opening!" he announces.

For the next twenty minutes hundreds of people stream into the stadium, slowly piling the seats with coats and bags and filling the air with chatter and noise, and then it's time to start. The tournament begins.

CHAPTER TWENTY-FOUR

**You always pass disappointment on the way
to the top. —Lucas Bailey**

**I always pass the Co-op on the way to
school. —Archie Crumb**

After a team talk from Mr Fell, we get into our positions
for the first match. The whistle goes. The other Archie
is in defence and he's so close to me it almost seems like
he's a second goalkeeper. I guess after the warm-up,
sir realized his mistake by having me as a sub in the
first place and told him to cover me. Ten minutes of
pretty decent football later we're celebrating. It's true
that I did not touch the ball once, but it still feels good
to hug and high-five everyone. No one mentions that
the other Archie basically was a keeper who could

only use his feet. I just stood next to him and shouted encouragement to everyone at the top of my voice.

"We can do this, lads!"

"YES! YES! WELL DONE!!"

"Great passing. Great teamwork."

"Believe in each other as much as you believe in yourself!"

I was definitely the loudest player on the pitch and the other team started telling me to shut up, so I just shouted even louder. The next three matches pass and we get into a good rhythm. Me shouting, the other Archie making saves, and Jayden and Dan scoring some incredible goals. The other Archie even lets me take a few goal kicks and pats me on the back when I get it past the halfway line. Cheers go up from the crowd every few seconds and even though the cheers are not all for us, it's nice to pretend they are. As I look around the pitch and see all of the teams and the crowds in the background, I smile to myself. It's nice to be part of something, to have so many people around me sending so much happiness out. It's like I can feel it in my body, making my head feel buzzy.

In between the matches I keep looking out into the crowd, my eyes searching to see if she's made it. Dan and Archie are on the phone to their mums and dads, trying to spot them waving in the crowd. Searching for their banners and red scarfs, leaping up and down with their arms in the air when they finally do.

The scary green-and-white team barge their way around the pitch closest to us. I can tell where they get their bruises from: they're brutal. Shoving kids out of the way with their shoulders and slide-tackling them to the ground. Not bothered by the yellow cards they keep getting. I really hope we don't have to play them.

Dan Dore scores so many goals and Jayden Thomas is playing really well too. The other Archie even takes the ball from the mouth of our goal when we are already winning one game 2–0 and scores an amazing goal in the top corner. Mr Fell's jumping up and down at the sidelines, shouting, "Yes, lads. Yes!" It starts to feel like we may actually be in with a chance. We easily make it through the group stages and into the quarter-finals. Now it REALLY matters. If we lose one game we're out.

The quarter-final is tough. The pitch is bigger and the game is longer. More of the crowd are focused on us and we can feel the pressure building. Dan and Jayden up front are just too good, and with me and Archie in the goal we manage to scrape through to the semis after a nervous twenty minutes.

After lunch it's the semi-finals and **everyone** will be watching. I totally forgot to bring any lunch and so Dan Dore has given me a banana and the other Archie gives me a biscuit. That's when it happens.

"He's here!"

Everyone slowly turns to see Lucas Bailey running out on to the pitch, followed by the rest of the team, all waving and high-fiving some of the kids. We drop our food and stand up to get as close as we can. As they do a lap of the pitch and head our way, I can feel everyone getting taller, standing on their tiptoes trying to become bigger, more noticeable. As he reaches us, he's waving over our heads to the crowds, who are all cheering like mad, and just as I think he is going to pass my outstretched palm he looks down at me. His eyes look straight into mine and he winks as if he recognizes me.

Maybe it really was him that night, I think. I take his sticker out of my pocket.

"I'm playing for you today, no wishes to help me along. I'm going to be the very best worst goalkeeper that I can be."

We look at the board to see who we're playing and thankfully the Mean Greens, as I'm now calling them, are in the other of the two semi-finals. If we win though, and they win, we will be playing them in the final. I can't think about that now. I just need to focus on the next game. The game that Lucas Bailey will be watching.

It starts off OK. We keep doing what we've been doing in the morning, the other Archie covering the goal with me and the others attacking well. No one manages to score and after half-time it's still 0–0.

Things start to fall apart as I see Lucas Bailey arriving at the sidelines, surrounded by TV cameras and jumping from foot to foot in his kit. It almost looks like he's about to join us on the pitch and I can't stop watching him. The other team are pretty good. When a tall girl with a swingy ponytail heads towards the box, I get myself ready to save. Then I hear Lucas's voice shouting, "Go on!" I don't know who he is talking to – me or the girl. I look over to see his face and then the other Archie shouts, "Archie!" As I twist around to see him, with my back to the pitch, the girl strikes the ball hard and it hits me right on the back of the head and bounces off up into the net. I don't know if you have ever had a football hit you hard on the head, but it feels like your brain has been knocked about. The rest of the team are groaning and have their heads in their hands and most of the crowd are either laughing at me and my dazed expression or cheering for the other team. The other Archie comes over and ruffles my hair.

"Sorry, pal, I shouldn't have shouted at you. I just didn't know if you'd seen it coming."

"It's OK. I hadn't," I say, feeling sorry for myself, but even sorrier for the rest of the team. We're now losing 1–0 in the semi-final and there are only five minutes of the game left.

As the game restarts, Dan Dore and Jayden quickly take the ball from the centre spot and head towards the other goal. They make it look so easy. Some people are like that, aren't they? The more pressure they're under, the stronger they get. Not me; I just crumble under pressure. I should be called Archie Crumble. They score a simple goal and high-five each other and then raise their arms to the crowd, demanding more cheers.

One minute later and they are back in front of the other keeper, passing it between themselves.

"You can do it!" I shout. "You're both awesome!" Dan dummies it and lets Jayden put it in the bottom left-hand corner. We're winning in the semi-final and there are only thirty seconds to go. Everyone seems to have forgotten about my own goal and I look over at

Lucas, who is rubbing his hands together and smiling.

When the referee places the ball on the centre spot I know that this is it; they are going to try their hardest to get a goal now. I focus on the ball. Ponytail girl immediately gets a pass and dribbles it straight towards me. I check that Archie is by my side and try to push down the panic that's rising in my chest. With only seconds left on the clock, she takes it past Kit and then strikes the ball hard and high. It sails through the air above the other Archie's head and as he realizes that it's heading into the net behind him, he raises his arm and the ball bounces off his outstretched fingers, up over the crossbar. I see his eyes close tight as he lands on the ground, knowing what he's done. The whistle blows and my heart sinks. Hand ball.

A penalty.

I CAN'T save a penalty, and the whole world, including Lucas Bailey, are about to watch.

The referee places the ball on the penalty spot and blows his whistle again. Ponytail girl looks at me and smiles. As though there is no chance on earth that I could save it.

Maybe there is a chance though – a tiny chance but a chance all the same. If the last few weeks have shown me something, it's that anything can happen, however small the chances. I clap my gloves together and imagine myself saving the ball. Maybe I CAN do this. Yes, I'm not the best footballer in the world, but I can save one penalty, surely. I've had enough practice in Mouse's back garden. It's just luck, choosing which way to jump and maybe getting it right.

She runs up to the ball and I see her eyes flick up to the top left and so I go for it. I stretch high, my arms reaching as far as they can, and as my eyes close, I feel the ball hit my gloves. I land on the ground with a thump and everyone piles on top of me. I did it, I actually did it. The crowd is cheering and the referee is blowing his whistle, trying to get some order so that we can finish the last few seconds of the game.

When the final whistle's blown a huge cheer erupts and I see the television cameras swooping around the sidelines. We are in the final! We did it! I did it! No magic, no wishes, just me. Archie Crumb.

We head over to our area and as I grab a drink of water, I can hear it in the background.

"ARCHIE! ARCHIE! ARCHIE! ARCHIE!!!" *I know that voice*, I think, and look up, scanning the crowds, and as I try and tune into the tiny chanting voice, I eventually see her.

"ARCHIE! ARCHIE! ARCHIBALD!!"

Scadge is waving her arms wildly and holding a piece of paper that says: WE LOVE YOU, ARCHIBALD. Next to her is my dad, who's smiling and waving. I wave back, looking to see if Mum is there.

How do they even know about this? They look so happy to see me, and before I can feel any anger towards my dad, I just feel pleased to have someone watching me. Someone who cares. As I am gathering my thoughts, another noise jolts me out of my confusion.

"KARGHH KARGHHH."

The squawk!

"Not bad, Arch!" says Mouse, grinning at me as I turn to see her. "I still think I should have been on the team, but not too crummy, Crumb."

"You made it!" I say, pulling her into a tight hug. "How are you here?"

"The second house cancelled. I was watching it all on telly when I saw you make the semis, I literally ran here non-stop. Sir saw me on the way to the toilet and said I could come and watch from here! He said that he was sorry for not putting me on the team, for not giving me a chance. Miss Crowther showed him the speech! Have you seen Lucas yet?"

"Yeah, he winked at me."

Then sir calls us all together and Mouse shouts good luck after me as I join the team.

"Right, lads, I think it's only right to leave this last team talk to the hero of the moment, Archie. What have you got to say to everyone, Arch?" I look over at the Mean Greens all barging each other about. I try to think of one of the sticker phrases but none of them seem quite right, so I just start talking.

"They're rough, this lot; they might even hurt us." I see the worried looks on people's faces, so I carry on. "If they knock you over, just keep getting back up. Show them that you won't let them bring you down. However tough something is, I know that we can be stronger. That's how we will win this, by not giving up." Everyone grabs each other into a back-slapping hug. Mr Fell pats me on the back and then finishes the team talk.

"I couldn't have said it better myself, Archie. We have got half an hour to drink some water and watch the Valley lads show us how it's done, then it's the final. Enjoy yourselves, you deserve it."

Lucas and the team head on to the pitch with the TV cameras circling, and loads of balls are thrown on to the pitch. They get into a formation and start by all keeping a ball up, and then, when a whistle blows, passing it around the circle to the next player. The way they control the ball, it's like a dance – it looks like it's attached to them and couldn't possibly hit the ground. The crowd are going mental, it's so loud. Then they line up and all take shots at the goal, doing rainbow flicks and overhead kicks and laughing at each other, making it more and more elaborate with each shot. Some balls go in and others fly high over the net, but they don't seem to care; they're just enjoying themselves and the crowd are loving it. When the show's over, someone runs on with a microphone and hands it to Lucas.

"Hello, Valley Stadium!" he calls. Huge cheer. "Thank you so much for coming today. It's been a brilliant day and has raised loads of money for children all over the country who don't have enough money to play sport, or even to buy enough food. By being here we are all helping." Another huge cheer. "I grew up down the road, and life was a bit of a struggle for me at times, but you know what? I got through it and I'm doing all right now!" Cheers and whistles. I am standing on my feet and clapping so hard that my hands are hurting. "I had people looking out for me and helping me get through, and so I want to make sure other kids have help too, because if you're having a tough time, sometimes just the smallest thing can make a difference. We've got to look after each other, ask for help when we need it, give each other hope, because if you've got hope, then you can get through anything. Good luck to the two teams in the final. Enjoy the show!" Massive cheers. Watching Lucas walk off the pitch, I feel like the speech was just for me, like the rest of the crowd were not even here.

I think about what a difference he has made to my life. Whether he was real or in my head that night when I fell off my bike, it doesn't really matter. He changed me. Made me think that I can make things happen – things that I never thought were possible. I want to do that for someone else one day. Be the one looking after other people, spreading hope. Helping people to keep going, even when it's hard. Obviously I can't do it as a footballer like Lucas, but maybe there are other ways. It feels good knowing what I want for the first time in my life. Knowing who I want to be.

First of all, though, I need to keep going, and that starts with playing the Mean Greens in the final at Valley Stadium.

CHAPTER TWENTY-FIVE

**I got through it and I'm doing all right now!
—Lucas Bailey**

**I've not got through it and I'm pooing my
pants. —Archie Crumb**

The Mean Greens look even scarier close up. They're
all massive, even bigger than the other Archie. The
game starts badly when a huge boy with a headband
shoulder-barges Dan to the ground. I see Dan trying
to pretend it didn't hurt when it clearly did.

"Don't let them get to you, Dan," I hear myself
shout. He gives me a brave smile.

By half-time it's still 0–0 and most people on the
team have been shoved or pushed and are feeling
tired and a bit sore. Even the crowd seem tired now

and aren't making so much noise. It's amazing how the Mean Greens seem to have sapped everyone's energy.

"Don't let them get to you, boys," Mr Fell tells us. "This is what they want. Keep your chin up. One goal could win this, just one."

In the second half, I can hear Mouse cheering, desperately trying to help us on. She wanted this so badly and deserved it more than anyone. Here she is cheering us on rather than doing it herself.

And then I realize: I can make her wish come true.

Just as the idea hits me, I see Dan Dore going up for a header and colliding with the much bigger head of the biggest of the Mean Greens. I know straight away that it's bad. The whistle goes and the ref holds up a yellow card as Dan writhes on the pitch in pain. I try to get sir's attention, but he is too busy shouting at the ref and gesturing for the first aid people. Dan comes off the pitch with his head in his hands and gets an ice pack. Brendan waits until the ref whistles him on to the pitch and the game carries on. It's useless; everyone is so tired there's no way we're going to score. Brendan is more of a defender and we have lost our highest-scoring player. When the final whistle goes and it's still 0–0, I know that it's time.

I run off the pitch and straight over to Mr Fell. After I've told him my plan, he goes over to the ref and I see the ref shaking his head, but then eventually they shake hands, smiling. When he comes back to our area, he whispers to me, "We're on! Get back in goal for extra time and I will get a spare kit ready. You're a team player, Archie, and a good friend."

Extra time seems to drag on for ever and with no one anywhere near scoring, we all know it's going to penalties. In the last minute, before Jayden takes a throw-in, the ref gestures to make a substitution.

Standing on the sidelines, fully kitted up and with the biggest grin on her face is Mouse, ready to take the best penalty Valley Stadium has ever seen. I take off my goalie gloves and hand them to the other Archie.

"Good luck, Archie," I say. "At least now you can save them with your hands as well as your feet!" I run off the pitch past Mouse, who calls out, "Thanks, Archie, you are the best."

When the penalties start, the Mean Greens suddenly look smaller somehow, now they can't push us around and it's just about goal-scoring skills. It seems obvious that we will win, we can all feel it, imagine it so clearly in our heads.

The Mean Greens are up first. Archie doesn't quite reach and it's a goal. Then Jayden blasts the ball into the top corner and we are neck and neck. Archie saves the next one, but Kit misses. The cries and cheers going up from the crowd feel as loud as they would if we were the Valley Squad in the play-offs. On the fifth penalty it's still neck and neck. Archie makes the most amazing save, stretching right across the goal, and it's now left up to Mouse. If she scores we have won the whole tournament. I think of all of the penalties I have ever seen her take. I KNOW she can do it. I look into her eyes. I can see her nerves but underneath I know that she believes in herself. She makes it look so easy, tricks the keeper into diving left and then taps it into the bottom right corner.

I run on to the pitch. The other Archie lifts me high into the air and then we both fall to the ground laughing. Mouse runs over and spins me round in a huge hug and then we look out into the cheering crowd and wave our arms to the sound of happiness.

When it's time to get our trophy, we all line up to shake Lucas's hand and have him put a medal around our necks. I'm at the back of the queue and can feel myself getting hot with excitement. When Mouse heads up for her medal and the others are all standing around the trophy, raising it into the air, I look around and think that this is perfect. I couldn't have even imagined this feeling, let alone wished for it.

As Lucas puts the medal around my neck, I look up and smile at him.

"Thank you," I say.

"You did so well out there. I'm proud of you. I bet you couldn't have wished for more, eh?" He winks down at me and laughs his warm laugh.

CHAPTER TWENTY-SIX

**I got through it and I'm doing all right now!
–Lucas Bailey**

**I got through it and I'm doing all right now
too! –Archie Crumb**

As me and Mouse are walking out of the ground into the car park, I see Scadge holding up her banner and waving at us. Behind them I can see an ice cream van – *my* ice cream van! When I get closer and see Martin looking through the hatch, he smiles and calls over,

"Archie! Do you think you are ready to face another ice cream yet?"

"I think I could give it a go," I call back, laughing.

Then Scadge runs towards me with her arms wide.

"You won, Archibald!! You were so amazing. It's been the best day of my life!"

"Well, thank you Scadge," I say lifting her up into the air and swinging her around. Dad stands watching awkwardly.

Martin gives us all double ice creams with sprinkles, and refuses Dad's offers to pay.

"Your boy is pretty special. He's got ice cream for life!"

"How's baby Archie?" I ask.

"The blighter never sleeps! I have to have naps in the van, like you, Archie!"

As we are walking away from the ice cream van, Dad looks at me and says, "What on earth have you been getting up to?!"

"It's a long story!" I say, winking at Mouse.

We stand and lick our ice creams and I look around for Mum but can't see her anywhere. Dad looks pretty uncomfortable and I can tell that he doesn't really know what to say next. Scadge rescues him.

"Who are you?" she asks Mouse, her eyes wide with the excitement of the day and her face now covered in ice cream.

"This is my friend Mouse."

"That's a cool name!"

I look at Dad and give him an awkward smile and he ruffles Scadge's hair and says, "Scarlett, why don't you go and show Mouse how you can dangle from the railings. I just need to chat to Archie for a minute."

"Come on, Mouse!" Scadge says, and leads her over to the railings, chattering the whole way. "Is Mouse your real name? I would love to be called Unicorn Sparkles the Third."

When they have got far enough away, Dad says, "That was amazing, son. I'm so glad I came."

"How did you know about it?" I ask.

"We went over to yours this morning, we've not seen you since... Anyway, your mum told us."

"So she didn't come too?" I say, suddenly feeling all of the excitement of the day drain out of me. Even though I couldn't see her out there, there was a tiny part of me still hoping. It was stupid. She's never going to get better.

"She wasn't feeling up to it, Arch. Listen, mate, the reason we came, we wanted to see you. Scadge has missed you and so have I. I've had time to think, buddy, and I just wanted to say that I'm sorry. I should have been better."

"Why weren't you, then?" I ask, and it sounds harsher than I mean it to.

He rubs his hand over his face. "Honestly, Archie, I don't know. I didn't know what you needed. Every time I saw you it reminded me of how useless I was being. It was easier to stick my head in the sand. Easier, but wrong." He takes a deep breath. "I'm sorry. So sorry, Arch. If you'll let me, I want to try again."

"I can't just go back to how it was. You can't cancel and 'rearrange' every time I'm meant to come over. It's not fair," I say.

"I know. I want to see you properly from now on. I want to look after you. You're my boy, Archie."

I think about Lucas's speech, about asking for help, and then I let it all out.

"Well, I need some school trousers that fit," I mumble.

"I can do that."

"I want to watch football on the telly with you again."

He smiles and I keep going.

"Oh, and if you have a spare laptop, then it would make doing the food shop and doing my homework a lot easier." Then things start tumbling out of my brain. Things that I want but have never asked for.

"I want my room at your house to feel like mine. I want to see Scadge and be her big brother. I want to be invited to things and do them as a family."

"Arch—"

"I'm not finished," I say. "I need you to remind me to wash my hair every now and then and to send me home with nice food. I need you to get the messages from school about sports days and school trips and deal with them." Then I take a big breath in and feel my chin wobble, but I keep going. "I want to come to yours *every* weekend instead of every other week, because Mouse is leaving and I don't have anywhere else to go and being at home with Mum since you left is hard. I love her but she is sad and poorly and I can't make her better and so I need you to look after me a bit more because she can't right now."

I look up at Dad and see tears streaming down his face. He is nodding and sniffing and he grabs me into a tight cuddle.

"Are you finished?" he says, into my hair.

"For now," I mumble.

"I'm so sorry, Archie. You've been doing the food shopping? Looking after yourself? Why didn't you tell me? I'm so sorry. Of course I can do all of these things."

I can feel tears rolling down my cheeks, but it feels different to the last time Dad made me cry. These feel like tears of relief, for finally figuring out – and asking for – what I really need. The things that will actually change my life. Forget about stickers and ice cream vans; these are the things that I didn't even know I was wishing for deep down.

When Scadge and Mouse come back, we wipe our eyes and Dad says, "Oh, yeah, Julie sent something for you too. I've no idea what it is, she wouldn't let me look." He puts a perfectly wrapped square box into my hands and says to Scadge, "Scarlett, or should I say Scadge, it's time to go, but Archie is coming over on Saturday morning!"

"Yes!!!" Scadge cheers, and wraps her little arms around me.

After waving Scadge and Dad off, me and Mouse head towards home.

"You were amazing, Mouse. What a penalty!"

"It was perfect, wasn't it? He had no chance!" she says, re-enacting kicking the ball and celebrating with her arms in the air.

We walk in silence for a while, both reliving the day in our heads, smiles on our faces and our hands occasionally touching the medals dangling from our necks. When we get to my street Mouse stops and turns to me.

"I didn't want to tell you today, but the house we looked at this morning was pretty amazing. Mum and Dad loved it. They put an offer in this afternoon and it was accepted straight away – that's the real reason we didn't go and look at the other house."

We stop walking and I stare at the ground, my eyes tingling. I pinch my lips together tightly.

"So that's that then?" I whisper.

"Kind of," she says. "There is good news though. Really good news."

"What?" I say, barely able to get the words out.

"The good part is that it's not as far as we thought and, because Dad will be driving in for work most days, they've said that I can finish year six at Valley Primary!"

It takes me a moment to process what she's saying.

"So you're not leaving school?!"

"Exactly!"

"So, I'll still see you every day?!"

That's when more tears spring out of my eyes and I just let them. I don't worry that I'm turning into my mum and I don't feel like they will never stop. These tears feel full of relief and happiness. I don't need to push them down or pinch them away.

"I'll have to kill some time after school every day until Dad's finished work, but that's no problem, is it – we've got our bus shelter and our wall!"

"I'll tell Mum that you are coming over to ours after school every day," I say, feeling my confidence growing. Asking Dad for everything that I need makes me realize that maybe I need to do the same with Mum. "It's my house too, and you and your mum have looked after me for so long. It's our turn to look after you a bit."

"Sounds good to me," she says, and then she adds quietly, "I've missed coming over to your house."

"Me too," I say.

I wipe my eyes and my breath stops jumping around. We start walking again.

"We'll go to different secondaries but we don't have to worry about that for now, do we?"

"No, I feel like I don't need to worry about anything now," I say. Even though Mouse is moving and nothing else has really changed, I feel different. Lighter. Then I turn to the house, think about going inside and have a sinking feeling. Of course I still need to worry about something. I don't want to go in; I don't want this perfect day where anything is possible to end.

"Who's the present for?" Mouse asks, gesturing to the gift that I totally forgot I'm holding. I unwrap the perfect paper and inside the box is the beautiful glass spray bottle, filled with Summer Breeze. I lift it up and inhale the perfect smell. Attached to the neck of the bottle is a little note which reads:

Let's make a fresh start.
    Julie X

Then the front door opens and my mum is standing there in her dressing gown, with a huge smile on her face.

"Are you coming in then? The two heroes of the day!"

"You saw it?!" I ask.

"Of course I saw it, I watched the whole thing. We were gripped, weren't we, ladies?" and as she opens the door, I see Zoe, Rosemary and Sir Lancelot sitting on the sofa.

"What's happening?" I whisper.

"It's been like Piccadilly Circus today, Archie. First your dad, then Rosemary and Zoe just arrived to tell me about the move. I'm exhausted, but you know what, sweetie? It's been the best day I've had in a long time."

"Me too!" I say, grinning.

"Well, come in, you two. Rosemary brought enough biscuits to sink a ship and I'm making cheesy pasta for tea. It's a mess, Mouse, which is why we have not had you round much, but, as I was just saying, maybe I need to start letting people in a bit more, and not just to the house either."

I go and help Mum with the cheesy pasta and leave Mouse eating biscuits in the living room.

As Mum's stirring the cheesy sauce and I get the plates out, it feels like I'm in a different house – a different life. Mum's still in her dressing gown and the house is still a tip, but I feel different.

"Thanks for making this, Mum. I love it so much."

Then she puts the spoon down and takes the sauce off the hob. She grabs hold of my cheeks with both of her hands, making my face feel all squashy, and looks me right in the eyes.

"I'm going to make some changes round here, Archie. What you said last night..."

"I'm sorry for shouting," I say.

"No, I needed it, Archie. I'm sorry. I've been talking today in a way that I've not spoken to anyone for a very long time. Rosemary's given me some numbers of people who I can ring. People who might help. It's not fair how much you've been doing. I'm sorry."

This time the sorry doesn't feel like it's going to lead to tears or bad memories. It's just matter of fact – the truth.

"I've been making changes too, Mum. I've realized I can't do it all on my own, so I'm going to start asking for help. I saw Dad and told him that he needed to do more – to be a better dad."

"Good on you, kid. You are a wise boy, that's for sure. I'm sorry that you've had to grow up so fast. I can't promise that I'll get better any time soon, but I *can* promise that I'll start talking a bit more, letting people help. Starting with Rosemary, who's offered to do the weekly shop for us! Bless her. So that's one less thing for you to do."

"As long as she doesn't forget the spaghetti hoops!" I say, and she ruffles my hair.

"Right, grub's up!"

I breathe in the smell of cheesy pasta and hear Rosemary, Zoe and Mouse playing with Sir Lancelot. It feels like a home again.

I smile to myself and whisper, "I didn't even wish for this." I must say it louder than I realize, as Mum turns and says, "You are not the only one who can make wishes, you know. What do you think I've been doing up in bed all this time?"

"Do you feel like your wish is coming true now too?" I ask.

"I tell you what I feel, Archie. I feel like it's time for me to stop just *wishing* and start *doing*."

"It sounds like it's coming true to me. I think sometimes you can make your own wishes come true."

"I think you're right, Archie – let's hope so."

After tea I show Mouse my room full of stickers, leaving Mum downstairs to say goodbye to Rosemary and Zoe. Mouse looks around at all the stickers and picks up a Lucas from my bedside table.

"Do you think it was magic or coincidence? I don't even know what would be weirder."

"Me neither," I say. "Maybe it was a bit of both. By me hoping and wishing for something, maybe I made it more likely to happen somehow."

"Maybe." She shrugs, and then she adds, "But what about when things don't come true? I wish for things all the time that never come true."

"Like what?"

"I usually wish that I could fly," she says.

"Well, maybe one day you will, but it might not happen in the way you imagine. Like, deep down, I was wishing that Mum would see me in the tournament – she didn't, not in the way I'd hoped, but maybe what's happened is even better. Maybe my wish came true in a way that I would never expect, but..."

"If you don't wish for it, it can't come true, can it?" we both say together, laughing. Then she starts running her hands through the sticker boxes.

"What are you going to do with all these?"

"Make my millions!" I say, and laugh an evil laugh.

"Don't you still have one left?" she asks.

"What?"

"A wish?"

"Yup," I say.

"So everything that happened today, us winning and me scoring, that was all real?"

"Totally real," I say, and we both sit there remembering every moment of the day, knowing that it was all very, very real.

"So ... I guess the big question is, did you really meet Lucas Bailey that night?"

"Who knows?" I say. "I think what I've realized is that it doesn't really matter either way. These things all happened, and whether it was because I started believing in magic, or even in myself a bit more, either way it's made me better."

"Better how?"

"I've got hope now. It's hard to be a good person if you don't have any hope. It's hard to be *anything* without hope. You end up like Mum in bed without it."

"Well, she's up now, isn't she?"

"Yeah, I think that it spreads – you can catch feelings. Just like you can catch sadness, you can catch hope. I think I'd caught a bit of Mum's sadness for a while. So, I'm going to try and hold on to as much hope as possible, now I've got it. Start using it to figure out what I need and then do something about it. If I can't change something then I need to ask for help."

"You know you can ask me and Mum for anything, Arch. She's been desperate to help for so long but never knew what to do. Just because we are moving that doesn't change."

"Thanks, Mouse, I will. I'm sorry I never really told you how bad things were."

"That's OK. I'm sorry that I didn't know how to keep asking."

It's getting dark and Mouse gets up to go. Then she stops.

"Oh, I almost forgot. Even though I'm not exactly 'leaving' you any more, I still want you to have something." She carefully opens her bag to reveal Flump sitting in a warm and cosy pocket. "She couldn't see much because she's too tiny. But you LOVED the tournament, didn't you, Flumpy?" she says as she holds her out to me.

"Imagine if she answered you back!" I laugh as I take Flump and give her a cuddle.

"I wish I was bigger!" I say in a squeaky Flump voice, looking into her tiny round eyes and picturing a humongous Flump. Imagining what she would say. "I wish me and all my rodenty mates were massive, like Mousasaurs – taking over the world!!" Me and Mouse laugh at my stupid voice, and at that moment there's a sudden breeze and the bedroom door slams shut with an alarming bang. Mouse jumps and lets out a little squeal.

She looks at me and says, "Oh no, Archie. What did you just say?"

"Just that I bet Flump wishes she was massive and..." My voice trails off. I look at Flump, who looks right back at me, and then I look at Mouse.

"OH NO!"

ACKNOWLEDGEMENTS

She believed she could, so she did. —Unknown

She sat and cried in a writing shed, distracted herself with unnecessary tasks, bought loads of rubbish online and after a few months somehow managed to write a book. —Helen Rutter

Thanks to the wonderful Lauren and Chloe who chatted through initial ideas and supported me throughout. I am so lucky to have you both – such a strong editing/agenting combo.

Big thanks to Jenny, Gen and Sarah for all of your editorial help.

Andrew and Liam, you are brilliant. I LOVE the artwork and amazing cover for this book, so thank you both and to everyone involved.

Harriet, thank you for your joyful emails and exciting plans: you are a star.

Everyone at Scholastic and Madeleine Milburn, thank you all so much.

Sue, Ken and Jools – thanks for reading a very early draft of Archie's story.

Thanks to Rob, Lenny and Cleo who put up with me reading out loud to them almost constantly. You are all so wonderfully enthusiastic and supportive, even when I clearly don't know what I'm doing! I love you all so much.

Finally, thanks to my mum. Jean the Bean. You showed me how to wish and how to hope. I know that not all of your wishes have come true yet, but because of you I learned how to go out there and grab hold of mine. So, thank you. x

CHAPTER 1

**The past, the present and the future walked
into a bar.
It was tense.**

Everything I say is important. Or at least, that's what
my mum tells me. Sometimes she makes me repeat it
out loud. It's embarrassing. Saying anything out loud
can be embarrassing when you're me.

That's what I'm doing right now. Practising. Over
and over, in the mirror. You'll find me here pretty
often; it's where I do most of my chatting. Watching
my eyes tighten to a close and my jaw tense up.

"M-m-my name is B-B-B-Billy Pliiimpton a-a-a-
and I have a stammer. My name is Billy Plimpton and
I have a stammer. My naaame is Biiiiilllly and I have
a s-s-s-s-stammer."

If I *don't* stammer when I'm saying it, I go bright red. Like I'm lying to my own reflection. If I do get stuck then I still go red because stammering at yourself feels stupid. But my speech therapist once told me to practise. So I do. A LOT.

I only say this particular sentence on my own in my bedroom and never to real people. I wish I never had to explain that I've got something wrong with my speech. It helps, though, when new people have already been told, so that they aren't left trying to figure out what's going on with me. Some people take ages. It's hard to watch them trying to control their expression. So much going on in their eyes. Wondering if it's all just a joke. I wish it was.

That's the other thing I practise. Jokes. I LOVE jokes. Using words differently. Surprising people with a punchline. Laughing at my own reflection.

"W-w-w-w-what diiid the llama say when he got kiiiiiicked out of th-th-th-the zoo? Alpaca my b-b-b-baaaags!"

How can I be funny if I can't even speak? It's not easy to tell a joke when you can't get the words out. I ruin my own punchlines. It's very annoying. I spend hours watching comedians on YouTube.

How smoothly they speak; how fast. The delighted audience. I try desperately to copy them.

It's not always obvious that I have a stammer. Sometimes it just sounds like a big pause and other times like I'm singing one word for a really long time for no reason whatsoever. Like I'm having a competition with myself to see how long I can draw one word out. This afternoon I got stuck on the words "lemon drizzle" for what seemed like for ever. We were talking about our favourite cakes. The amount of time it took me to say it almost made me go off lemon drizzle cake a bit. Sometimes the words themselves annoy me, when I get stuck badly, like they are doing it on purpose.

My little sister Chloe's friend Aisha was over for tea today. They galloped around the kitchen making *clip-clop* sounds. Chloe's obsessed with ponies. Her room makes me feel sick, there are so many stuffed toy ponies everywhere and horse posters on the walls. I'm a bit scared of horses, but I would never tell her that. So I just don't go in there very often.

Aisha hadn't been to our house before. As we were eating our tea, I was singing my way through a new joke – "Wh-wh-wh-which hand is it better to write wiiiith?" – when Aisha asked, "Why do you talk like that?" As blunt as that, looking right at me over her forkful of spaghetti.

So Chloe explained for me: "He gets stuck on his words. He knows what he wants to say but his brain won't let it come out properly. You just have to wait until he's finished."

Aisha thought about it for a while, then sucked up her spaghetti and said, "I like it!" So that was nice. She also laughed at my punchline: "Neither, it's b-b-b-best to write w-with a pen!" which was even nicer.

At least Aisha was honest and just asked me the question. Kids are a bit better than grown-ups when they first meet me. They either ask straight out about my stammer, like Aisha, or just completely ignore it. That's the best, when someone doesn't even seem to notice and just waits till I'm done, knowing that I will get to the end eventually. Mum says a lot of the world's problems are caused by everyone being in such a rush and that I'm doing everyone a favour by forcing them to be a little bit more patient.

It's only when kids know what's going on with me that the problems can start. When they realize they can use it against me or laugh at me. Most of the time I just catch kids pulling funny faces at each other or giggling behind their hands as I am trying to say something. But just asking a question about it like Aisha did, that's fine. I would rather that than deal with the frowny/smiley face that adults have when I first speak to them. An upturned mouth and a wrinkled forehead. I hate it when people look at me like that. I want to make people smile properly, not in the frowny way. I can see the moment when it clicks. When they get it, that what they are hearing is a speech impediment and not a choice. They almost look relieved, pleased with themselves. Then they get to show off how good they are at dealing with such a thing. In my experience there are four main categories of grown-ups:

1. The Encouragers

They have calm, smiley expressions and constantly say things like, "Go on", "Interesting" and, "I understand." Encouragers are OK. Although they can be annoying when they go too far and say things like, "Take a big breath in," and, "Relax." Telling someone to relax when they are clearly struggling is like shouting, "Run faster!" at someone being chased by a tiger. They would if they could.

2. The Mind Readers

This is the most common category and a very annoying one in my opinion. A lot of adults do this to kids anyway, even kids without a stutter, but they REALLY do it to me. This is the category who think they know exactly what I'm trying to say and so "helpfully" finish my sentence for me. They usually say something completely wrong. Most of the time I just go along with their version of the conversation, because I can't be bothered trying again. I ended up going to the toilet once, when I didn't even need a wee. The lady at the cinema ticket office obviously thought I was going to ask, "Can you tell me where the toilets are?" when I was actually trying to say, "Can you tell me where the popcorn is?" She took me right to the toilets, even though there was a huge sign and an arrow, so I thought I should go in. I didn't even end up buying any popcorn. I told Mum I had changed my mind when I slid back into my seat and she called me a "strange fish". That's the other thing that happens when you have a stammer. People think you're either thick or strange.

3. The Jokers

The most upsetting category. The grown-ups who don't know what to do and so choose to mimic me "as a joke". Believe me, this happens more than you would think. The other day I went to the shop and had to ask an old man in a brown cap to reach the chocolate milkshake for me. He responded by saying, "Y-y-y-y-y-yes, of course I can!" and then laughed at how funny he thought he was. I'm not sure why any grown-up would do this. It's almost too confusing to be upsetting. I still felt bad, though.

4. The Waiters

The best category and the one which you should try and be a part of, should you meet a stammerer. These are the rare people who don't mind waiting and will stay there for as long as it takes for me to spit out whatever piece of information I'm stuck on. Usually a new joke. You could be waiting a long time until I get to the end of a new one-liner. That's kind of how it works. The more I want to say something, the less my voice allows me to say it. It's like a sick joke in itself.

Obviously some Waiters are not so good. You wouldn't believe how obvious it is when someone's waiting but they don't really want to be. That's tough. I want to say to them, "Don't worry. Just go and do whatever it is that you would rather be doing. This is no fun for either of us." But I don't, as that would take even longer than whatever it is I'm stuck on.

As I turn back towards the mirror for another attempt – "My name is B-B-B-B…" – Mum pops her head round the door.

"Who are you talking to, Billy?" she asks.

"N-N-No one," I say, pointing to my reflection.

"Gosh, if only that mirror could talk. It must have heard all sorts from you!"

"Wh-wh-what's said to the m-m-mirror, stays in th-the m-mirror, all right?" I say in my best gangster voice. Mum's a pretty good Waiter. I suppose she has had plenty of practice.

"Well, you and your mirror can carry on chatting for ten minutes, then it's bed, OK? It's a big day tomorrow, you need your sleep." She winks at me and her head disappears from the doorway. If only I could be normal then starting Bannerdale High School would be easy. I'm going to try everything I can think of to get rid of this stammer, and become just like everyone else. Maybe even better than everyone else. Imagine that, I could be the most popular boy in school.

"You know that Billy Plimpton, he's the best and he's SO funny."

"Yes, everyone wants to be friends with Billy Plimpton. I think he's going to be famous."

"Tell us another joke, Billy, go on!"

Everyone will crowd around me at lunchtime, desperately wanting to be my friend, eagerly listening to my jokes ... if I can get rid of my stammer. I don't want to think what it will be like at Bannerdale if I can't.